KALPAR

Ephemera

First published by Ironhammer Publishing 2025

Copyright © 2025 by Kalpar

First edition

ISBN: 978-1-962547-07-9

Editing by Isabella Betita
Cover art by Draya Brogden-Hughes

This book was professionally typeset on Reedsy.
Find out more at reedsy.com

*To the Trans Community and the Woke Agenda.
We deserve something nice.*

Contents

Acknowledgments

This book almost didn't happen. In 2024 my spouse and I bought a house and between that and *gestures vaguely* everything else, our finances got precarious enough that I could not fund this book on my own. Fortunately, thanks to twenty-six amazing people who backed the Kickstarter, I was able to raise enough money to get this book edited and into your hands. Those people are true heroes of this book and I want to thank them individually for their contributions to art in this, the darkest timeline.

Matthew, Revel, Erin, Pam, Rachel, Ben, Kris, Jessica, Anna, Amanda, Kelli, Allison, Emily, Bethanie, Jenna, Adam, Susan, Bob, Dash, Brooks, Maddie, Kristin, Chase, and Alexander, you are all amazing patrons of the arts and I hope that you love this book you helped make happen. To Uncle Alex and my spouse Peabody, thank you so much for continuing to financially support this crazy art I keep making. We haven't turned a profit yet, but maybe next year…

As always, thank you to my amazing editor, Isabella Betita. You always point out my blind spots, help make my clunkier sentences better, and metaphorically smack my hands when I should put an em dash in instead of an ellipses. To be fair, I overuse ellipses. Blame my love of *Star Wars.*

The song *Rocket Rider's Prayer* would not get out of my head and I *had* to incorporate it into a sci-fi story somehow. My eternal thanks goes to the song's author, Steven Savitzky, for his generous permission to include excerpts of the song in my story *A Matter of Protocol*. You can find Steve's collected works on his website https://steve.savitzky.net/ or you can follow him on Mastodon at ***@ssavitzky@indieweb.social***

A special thanks goes to my friend Draya who not only produced the beautiful cover art, but also provided the inspiration for the character of the Teal Witch. I have a couple more adventures for them, Anise, and Arty planned I hope you don't mind. Thank you to my friend girl!Jamie, that game of *Fiasco* we played however many years ago was a direct inspiration for *A Matter of Protocol*. Captain White borrowed your name for a bit, but he won't be using it anymore. Also thank you to Audrey Rodriguez and Pearson, who provided both names and inspirations for minor characters in *Stolen and Broken Hearts*. I hope you enjoy your roles. Finally, thank you to all of my enemies, you provided *so much* material.

And of course, thank you to everyone else who cheered me on. The Discord members who were excited by every writing update. The followers on Facebook, BlueSky, and Tumblr who loved the updates as well as the memes. (I'm so glad all you Tumblr people are just as *normal* about Murderbot as I am.) Every person who came to the events and bought something to help keep me going or said hi at the table. As my friend Laser advised I make this art primarily for me, but I'm so glad all of you enjoy it too.

Ghosts of Eddy

"I'm not used to this much of an audience when I'm abseiling." The ink must have still been drying on his doctorate because the spelunking archaeologist Joedii had shipped in looked absurdly young to be doing something this dangerous. "You ready on your end?"

"All good, you can start at any time."

His belayer started letting the rope out and the climber disappeared beyond the lip of the shaft. Nearly everyone on the two hundred-person expedition team, from the most senior archaeologist to their most novice cook, was in the cavernous room surrounding the main shaft. Everybody wanted to be able to say they had been there the day the real secret was uncovered. Dafnii stepped forward to the railing and watched as Maht descended in a controlled fall, dropping out of the range of the actinic floodlights mounted at the corners of the shaft. Soon he was only visible because of his oil headlamp, shrinking into the depths.

"How much length does he have on that rope?" Dafnii asked.

"Over two hundred meters on that one," Joedii, leader of the expedition, answered. "We've got longer ones if we need them, but I sincerely hope we don't." Everyone waited in silent anticipation as the belayer continued to slowly let out the rope through the pulley, which despite its ominous squeaking Joedii had been assured was capable of holding five hundred kilograms. Eventually the pull on the rope stopped, but it remained taut.

"Maht, how you doing, buddy?" the belayer shouted down into the depths and waited. Maht's response came back after a brief delay, echoing from the shaft's walls. "I'm okay. I *think* I see the bottom but it still looks pretty far away. I figure we've already let out about a hundred meters, what do you think?"

"I agree with you, about a hundred meters. You want me to pull you back up?"

"Yeah, I don't think I'm going to make it with this rope. Go ahead and bring me back up."

"Copy that, pulling you up now." Two more people came forward and started helping the belayer pull the rope back up. Most of the spectators turned away and started leaving the room, losing interest now it was clear nothing more interesting was happening today. Joedii let out a sigh. "Well, now we know it's at least three hundred meters down. I'll let the climbers figure out the details."

"Hey, Maht, you okay? We're getting some resistance on the rope." The rope audibly creaked; the belaying team stopped pulling on the rope but kept it taut.

"Yeah, I think it got snagged on something in the shaft. Let me kick out from the wall and see if that pulls it free."

"Everybody stand by!" the belaying chief shouted and took up her position at the front of the team, letting out a little bit of slack on the rope, which twitched as Maht kicked free into the air. The team grunted and pulled, but the rope refused to pull in further. The chief called down to Maht, "You want us to give you another five meters of slack and see if you can shimmy it loose?"

"Hang on, I think I felt something pull loose, let me try kicking out again." The rope pulled taut again and everyone could hear Maht grunt with effort. Then, there was an audible snap. The entire belaying team staggered back as the rope went limp, Maht's weight on the other end clearly gone.

"Maht, you okay?" There was a sickening thud from a very long distance away, and then silence."Maht? Maht?!" The belaying team frantically pulled on the rope but the squeak of the pulley now seemed mocking, the laughter of an ancient god that has exacted its blood sacrifice from the unwary. Grimacing, Dafnii and Joedii carefully looked over the edge of the shaft. Somehow Maht's oil lamp had survived the drop, but its flickering circle of light at the bottom revealed a growing pool of blood which meant Maht certainly hadn't.

"If I wasn't going down there before, I owe it to him to get down there now." Joedii's face was grim. "But before that, I want to know what happened." She stalked over to the belaying crew, two of whom were still staring, aghast, into the shaft. The chief was pulling the rest of the rope in without much enthusiasm. Soon, the severed end of the rope wound its way through the pulley, and she looked at the end, holding it pensively in her hands."It was cut clear through. He should have had a safety line, or we should have stopped him…" She looked ready to break into tears. "Oh, Maht…"

"We'll bring him back. And we're not going to lose another person doing it." Joedii's resolve was as solid as the granite monoliths that surrounded the building. "I don't care what it takes."

Two Weeks Earlier

"The preliminary excavations have been going very well. We've identified the outlines of a surface structure, although we're still debating as to its purpose. Personally, I suspect it was ritualistic in nature, but that will depend on what we find in the adjoining substructures. It's hard to imagine anything practical that people might have put all the way out here." She stopped talking as she took a swig from her canteen.

Joedii was tanned from the desert sun and all lean muscle from a lifetime of digging. Her career had begun as an undergrad, doing the unglamorous work of shifting wheelbarrows of sand as her superiors sifted through to find artifacts of ancient cultures. She'd paid her dues over the years, slowly climbing the hierarchy of academia from grad student to doctoral candidate to the elevated position of Ph.D., all while playing the cutthroat game of academic politics. After twenty years, this was the first dig where she and she alone was in charge and it would make or break her career as an archaeologist.

"What makes you think ritualistic?" Dafnii, on the other hand, had the pale look of someone more used to the dim recesses of a research lab's interior than the brightness of the sun. It was the excitement of Joedii's reports and the sheer magnitude of the dig that had lured Dafnii away from her precious artifacts and into the field.

"It's the monoliths mostly, there are hundreds of them all over the place. We're still trying to decipher some of them but they appear to have been inscribed in dozens of languages. There are a few that look related to languages we know, but in very, very archaic forms. The rest, I haven't a clue what they could be. That's part of why I wanted you to come out here, you've always been a much better hand at languages than I have."

Joedii led Dafnii over to one of the massive monoliths. "We found the first ones around the perimeter of the site. They appear to be made from local granite, but the level of detail implies whoever did this invested considerable time and effort into setting them up. Fortunately, the environment has gone a long way towards preserving the inscriptions, but that may just be an accident of environment. Deserts have always been an archaeologist's friend."

Dafnii brushed a hand over the face of the monolith, jutting like a finger from the ground. "It's incredible," she whispered, feeling the inscription with her fingers. "How many languages have you identified?"

"At least a hundred, although our field researchers aren't sure if some of them are dialects of closely related languages. Most of them we still haven't identified."

"What have you found?"

"Old Mandarin, Proto-Cyrillic-Asian, and what appears to be a very archaic version of Hindi."

"Oof, of course you'd give me Proto-Cyrillic-Asian. Well, Old Mandarin's probably the easiest since the ideograms only evolved gradually. Let me see what you've got."

Joedii pointed to one of the monoliths, at an inscription towards the base. Dafnii squatted down and squinted at the carving.

"This location is a message, part of many messages, take heed! Delivering this message was important to us, a powerful people. We do not honor this place, no great deed is remembered here, no treasure is here. What is here is repugnant and anathema to us. Heed our warning of this danger." Dafnii broke off reading.

"It gets more specific from there, something about where the danger is located and directions to it. I have to say, this is all very confusing. If they hated this place so much, why leave so many markers around?"

"That's what's been puzzling me. The Proto-Cyrillic-Asian and Hindi all appear to say something similar. 'This is a message, this place is dangerous, keep out.' Kind of makes me wonder what the hell they were hiding here. If you keep your mouth open like that, flies will find their way in." This last comment was directed towards Dafnii, who was sitting absolutely stunned.

"You don't think we've found another Rosetta Stone, have you? The implications could be… If nothing else this could be the biggest archaeological find of, well, the past thousand years at least." Joedii's secrecy and urgency made all sorts of sense in light of this fact. A find of *this* magnitude? It practically guaranteed becoming the next patron saint of archaeology, to say nothing of never having to fight for funding ever again.

"Boggles the mind, don't it? You want to see the main complex?"

* * *

"You know, based on everything surrounding this, I was expecting something more impressive. Whoever built this had a terrible sense of aesthetic style to say the very least. It just looks like…boxes."

Dafnii wasn't wrong. The structure consisted entirely of rectangular shapes that had been crammed together into a collective building. The walls were made of beige bricks that blended into the desert landscape.

"I have to admit, a lot of us felt the same sense of disappointment. I've seen a lot of buildings in my life, but this is probably the ugliest by far. Don't worry, it's a lot more interesting on the inside."

As ugly as the building was, it looked like it might be able to take a direct artillery strike, and in all honesty the building was probably built to survive exactly that. The doors were big, steel, and very much of the "built to keep people out" variety. One of the doors had been pried open, although the scorch marks from a small dynamite blast implied it hadn't been an easy process.

"I know, I know," Joedii said defensively. "It's not good archaeological practice, but can you blame us? Just the size of this thing alone is impressive."

The interior, at first, was just as unimpressive as the exterior, decorated in the same shades of desert beige. The corridors were dreadfully utilitarian but of a tremendous scale. "I just don't understand why a civilization would build something this big and make it this butt ugly. I mean, we have studied digs going back thousands of years on every continent, and never in my entire life have I seen something quite as ugly as this."

"I've seen pictures of some things that were almost as bad, can't say I've heard of anyone finding an example of one that still existed. Do you think this could be from the same civilization? They seemed to specialize in architecture designed to bore people away." Dafnii let the light from her lantern play across the walls, illuminating more signs on the walls. "Here, look at these!"

Joedii stopped her walk into the building and joined Dafnii "These are even weirder than the ones outside. What do you think, pictograms?"

"That's my guess. It looks like a person running away from something but I have no idea what this symbol here means."

Dafnii pointed towards a trefoil-shaped symbol with rays emanating from it. "I don't know what this could represent, the sun, maybe? If they built this place as a refuge from the outside environment? That doesn't make a lot of sense, though. I wish I knew what these inscriptions here meant." There was writing beneath the pictograms but it was in one of the many languages that had been lost to time. "You said the really interesting thing was further inside?"

"Down this way." Joedii walked through another enormous doorway and her lantern disappeared into a truly enormous room. "I think this is the central box that we saw from the out-side. It's the only thing that could contain this much volume." They stared up into the cavernous room; chains dangled from the ceiling and catwalks led to bulks of machinery, looming like gargoyles from the heights. The center of the room was surrounded by a fence, enclosing a perfectly square perimeter.

Curious, Dafnii walked forwards and grew confused as the area within the fence remained dark, as if the light of her lantern was swallowed by some entity. She only understood once she reached the fence and looked down. And down. And down. After a good minute her brain finally managed to start working again. "It's a shaft. It's like a mining shaft going straight down. You have any idea how far down this thing goes yet?"

"Not yet," Joedii's voice echoed from the walls. "We're waiting to get the right equipment and some experienced spelunkers out here first. I was actually surprised by the amount of overlap between archaeologists and spelunkers. If everything goes well we'll have the people and equipment on site sometime next week. In the meantime, I'd like you to try and decipher as much of this writing as possible to see if we can get an idea of what we might encounter down there."

Dafnii stepped back from the shaft. "It certainly raises more questions. My gut tells me this is a mining complex, the incredibly basic to butt-ugly architecture would match with a purely industrial installation. But then why all the monoliths around the complex? It seems the more we learn about this place the less sense it makes."

"You and me both."

* * *

"If everything goes well, we're going to send the first team down tomorrow. I'm hoping we'll hit the bottom but that might be too optimistic." Joedii plopped down into the empty camp chair across from Dafnii. The table was covered with rubbings of the engraved monoliths, and Dafnii's notations filled the margins in her cramped handwriting. "Any luck with the translations?"

"Well, the first part seems pretty consistent. Statements that this is a message, take heed of it, we are a powerful people. But I'm still utterly confused as the message continues. It warns of a great danger in this location and says it's capable of killing and we should shun this location. But it's vague as to what the danger is, I can't quite make out the words."

"That's frustrating. For something this supposedly dangerous, you'd think they'd be more specific about what the threat actually is. You don't think this could be a funerary curse like you sometimes see in tomb complexes? You know, to ward off grave robbers?"

Dafnii leaned back and rubbed her eyes. "As entertaining as that might be, my gut reaction to that is no. This structure looks far too…industrial. Tombs almost always involve some sort of decoration or embellishment, even the poorest people try to leave something. Aside from all the warnings and signs, we haven't found anything that looks like a proper name, which you'd expect in a tomb. My conclusion is whoever built this place thought they'd left something dangerous here and wanted everyone to know about it."

"That makes a certain kind of sense," Joedii said. She leaned over to her own camp desk and pulled out a geographic survey. "The records are fragmentary but it looks like we're on top of a massive salt dome. One of the geologists said that when you get enough rock salt somewhere it becomes impervious as long as it stays dry. Maybe they put something in the bottom of a salt mine?"

"That would certainly go with the industrial look of the place," Dafnii agreed. "But that still begs the question of what could be so dangerous you buried it in a salt mine?"

"Well, we won't know until we get down into that mine shaft and check. Or if you find anything more specific from these inscriptions."

"I'll try my best. Anybody have any more guesses on the pictograms?"

"Not yet. Aside from the usual rude suggestions."

* * *

"They're bringing Maht up tomorrow," Dafnii said. "Thought you might want to be there, considering." It had been two weeks since Maht's untimely demise and everyone had been in a sour mood since. The excitement of the initial discovery had been overshadowed by the accident. There was an awkward pause, as if someone wanted to say something but was too afraid to say it. Joedii glowered at Dafnii.

"What is it?" she asked gruffly. Her attitude had changed more dramatically than anyone else on the expedition, quicker to anger and far less jovial. She was no longer the affable dig leader, making sure everyone was drinking enough water. Now she was more like a bitter, disappointed parent, ready to find fault with any mistake no matter how trivial. Dafnii had seen grad students shrink in fear as Joedii stomped about the site, hoping they could avoid her ire for another day.

"It's just… A lot of us are thinking maybe we should leave well enough alone once we bring Maht back up. We've already made history with what we've found, maybe we should just…"

"We're not abandoning the project!" Joedii shouted, rising from her chair. "I fully intend to go down there and find out what's so damn important about this place." Dafnii backed away as Joedii stormed towards her until she was against the wall, Joedii's finger poking into the center of her chest. Dafnii cowered under Joedii's assault. "I'm in charge on this dig, I'll say when we're done."

"There's a lot of talk in camp that this whole place is cursed. Some of the spelunkers are refusing to go back down the shaft. Everybody knows about the translations of the monoliths, what if there really *is* a curse? I mean…"

"Don't tell me you've fallen for that load of superstitious crap! We're scientists, for crying out loud! Are we going to let the primitive beliefs of some culture dead a thousand years or more keep us—modern, enlightened, rational people—from advancing knowledge? We don't know *anything* about this civilization. If we just give up now it's…." Joedii sputtered incomprehensibly with her frustration and rage.

"I understand," Dafnii soothed. "But a man's already died. Maybe it's time to go back, ask for some more funding, make sure we do this properly."

"You think they'd let a couple of next-to-nobodies like ourselves keep running this dig if we go back for funding, especially after someone's already died? Every archaeology department at every university in the civilized world is going to be competing to dig here! Not to say when the local government gets involved."

She couldn't let it end here, she *couldn't*. This was *her* dig and she owned everything about it. She could go home to the university with a partial success, but she *knew* the department chairs would see it as a failure. "Not ambitious enough." "Doesn't have the stomach for it." "Lacking in leadership." Those sorts of comments would follow her record wherever she went and she'd spend the rest of her life digging up potsherds for someone half as intelligent as her but better-connected.

No, she *needed* to see this through. "I am going to the bottom of that shaft tomorrow and finding out what's so damn important about this place. You can either come down with me, or run back to your laboratory and translations." Joedii turned and stormed out of the tent, leaving behind a speechless Dafnii.

* * *

High above, the mule-powered winch creaked into action and the mining cage began climbing back up the shaft. Maht's body had begun to desiccate due to a combination of the heat and the rock salt that made up the floor of the shaft. It had reminded her a little of the two mummies she'd been fortunate enough to examine. There was still a patch of salt stained dark red where Maht's blood had spilled and she tried to avoid stepping on it when she had stepped down from the cage. Dafnii frowned as the cage ascended out of the zone of torch-light established at the bottom of the shaft.

"You okay?" one of the excavators asked. He was a big, burly man whose muscles testified to years of physical labor. Dafnii recognized him as one of the mining experts that Joedii had rushed in and forced to sign intimidating non-disclosure agreements. They hadn't asked too many questions and good wages bought plenty of silence, but it was clear this man was starting to think maybe they should have asked a few more questions before agreeing to this job.

"Just have a very bad feeling about this." Dafnii shuddered. "I keep thinking about what happened to Maht and wondering if the rope on that cage will get cut in half too."

The excavator nodded with understanding. "We think his rope got caught on one of the steel supports in the shaft. Quite a few have a razor edge on them. How I don't know, but you've got nothing to worry about there. That cable is over ninety strands of eight gauge steel wire wound around each other. Nothing's cutting through that."

"That's…reassuring," Dafnii said. "Although to be honest this place gives me the heebie jeebies."

"Ah yes, the heebie jeebies, very technical term." The excavator laughed reassuringly. "Run into in mines all the time, but trust me you got nothing to worry about. We've got the latest safety equipment and salt? Seals everything tighter than my dearly departed granny's canning. We don't have to worry about firedamp down here." He looked ready to say more but Joedii interjected.

"Come on, I want these seals opened." She stood with her arms crossed, tapping her foot impatiently. "We've already done proper documentation on this one." She jerked her head towards one of the tunnels branching out in four directions from the central shaft. The tunnel was sealed with a massive concrete plug and covered in yellow signs.

The excavation team entered the tunnel with a variety of crowbars, hammers, and other tools and attacked the concrete face with gusto. "You're still not having second thoughts about this, are you?" Joedii asked.

"Do the sheer quantity of these concern you at all?" Dafnii gestured towards the yellow signs that the excavation team had already removed from the tunnel and were stacking in the central shaft. "The language of the signs has only gotten more strident the further into the complex we've gone. Warning about death, some sort of spirit that can kill, a terrible curse that still lives in this place."

"Superstitious nonsense!" Joedii practically spat the words out. "Who knows what sort of belief system these people had?"

"We're not talking about some civilization that thought a piece of bread turned into their god and then ate it! The people who built this place had complex tools and planned for this place to be here for centuries. Surely we should at least *consider* that there's some danger?"

There was a loud crack and both women turned to see the concrete plug broken into a pile of rubble. "It looks like we're clear through to the other side!" the foreman shouted. "Give us a minute to shift this and the whole tunnel will be clear."

Joedii picked up her lantern and immediately clambered over the pile of rubble, refusing to even wait for the excavators to finish their work. "Come on, Dafnii! I'm going to need you to do any translations." Reluctantly, Dafnii grabbed her own lantern and followed into the tunnel. The room beyond was filled with large, white cylinders twice as tall as a person and so wide around it would have taken four or more people with arms outstretched to encircle one.

"Do you know what these markings mean?" Joedii pointed the light towards the cylinders, focusing on a short string of symbols in black that was the only marking on the canister.

"The symbols look like they repeat," Dafnii said. "I'm not sure of the significance, though. It could represent a great number of things."

Joedii walked up and rapped on one of the canisters and it gave a deep metal ring. "Sounds like they're hollow. What do you think about this?" She pointed to a silver band around the circumference of the canister, about two-thirds up the structure. "Looks this could be where the lid sealed on? Maybe if we rig up a pulley." The top of the canister nearly brushed the ceiling. "Guess we'll have to drag it out into the main shaft to get the clearance…"

"I guess," Dafnii conceded. "Look, do we really want to be poking around in these? I mean, who knows what they could contain?" She shone her lantern deeper into the cavern and row after row of canisters reflected the light back. "God knows there's certainly a lot of them down here."

"Makes you wonder what's in all of them. We could spend years cataloging everything!" Joedii's enthusiasm seemed utterly inappropriate for the sepulchral atmosphere of the cavern. "Hey, guys!" she shouted back. "You got some dollies or jacks or something?! Getting a mule team would probably be ideal but I don't know if we could get them down here.

Maybe we could improvise some rollers…" Dafnii seemed about to protest, but she quickly accepted that Joedii was beyond listening to any counterarguments.

In less time than Dafnii thought was possible, the excavators had pulled one of cylinders out of the tunnel and into the central shaft. It took even less time for them to rig a cable through the lid of the canister and link it with the hoist at the top of the shaft. With a groan, the lid came free, revealing what treasures were hidden inside.

"It's just more canisters?" Joedii climbed up the canister and looked inside, clearly disappointed. "That just doesn't make any sense. Why put more canisters inside of canisters? That makes absolutely no sense."

"Ritualistic, do you think?" Dafnii couldn't resist making the joke, but Joedii was in no mood.

"It makes no goddamn sense. Why go to all this effort? Crowbar!" She whirled and extended her hand expectantly. After some shuffling about the excavators finally handed her a crowbar and she attacked one of the smaller canisters. With a loud clang, she managed to pry the lid off and open the container.

"It's just…metal." She reached in and lifted out a rod of silvery metal. "It's heavy, warm too. That's weird. Why is it— Ahhhhhh!" Joedii's train of thought cut off with a scream as she dropped the metal back into the canister. "Sonofabitch! It burnt me! What the hell *is* this?"

Members of the excavation crew joined Joedii and looked into the canister. "I've worked in metal shops before," one of the crewmen said, "but I can't say I've seen any metals that act like that. It's damn odd. Come on, ma'am, we better get that hand looked at. This will keep for a little longer."

They were about halfway up the shaft in the lift cage when Joedii moaned and sank to her knees. "I don't feel well at all, I feel like…" She let out a desperate sound, and then Joedii began vomiting desperately. Dafnii winced as bile fell through wire mesh and splattered below.

"Joedii, are you okay?" Dafnii realized the futility of her statement as she made it. For all its versatility, human language always failed in moments of crisis. She wrapped an arm around Joedii and managed to fumble a handkerchief out of her pocket, trying to clean up Joedii's face with a modicum of success. "What's wrong? Talk to me, Joedii."

"I don't… I feel so nauseous and I…" She moaned again and her explanation was interrupted by more vomiting and a series of dry heaves. Dafnii did her best to hold back Joedii's hair as the woman shook. "I feel so weak all of a sudden. I don't understand."

"Is everyone okay?" a voice called down from the top of the shaft and the lift cage stopped, creaking on its cable.

"No, we've got a bit of a situation down here! Joedii needs medical attention right now! Keep lifting us up!" Panic and desperation filled her voice. "Please, we need to get her back up right away." The person at the top of the shaft didn't bother to respond, but the mule team went into action again. "It'll be okay, Joedii." Dafnii knelt next to Joedii and made an ineffectual effort to comfort her. "We'll get you some help. Soon as we can. It'll be okay."

* * *

"She's still got a fever and the vomiting and diarrhea hasn't gone down. I've been keeping he hydrated but without a doctor, there's not a whole lot I can do out here in the field. I'm thinking we need to send her to a hospital soon." The medic blinked in the sunlight outside the tent, where they'd laid up everyone who'd fallen ill since opening the cavern.

"If she can survive the journey," Dafnii said doubtfully. "How are the rest of them?"

"Mixed. Some of them have recovered, some are in as bad condition as Joedii. The symptoms all seem to be similar. Fever, vomiting, diarrhea. It doesn't appear to be contagious for now at least, but it's probably best to keep everyone quarantined. And I don't want anybody else going down that mine shaft. I don't know if it's bad air, a curse, or some supergerm trapped down there for a thousand years. So far you're the only person who hasn't caught whatever this is."

"I'll tell Joedii's second-in command," Dafnii said. "Although at this point I don't think anybody is lining up to head down there."

"Whole damn place is cursed, should have listened to the markers." The medic tapped out a cigarette and paused before she lit up. "Oh, Joedii wanted to talk with you. She's conscious for now, but probably not much longer."

Dafnii ducked into the infirmary tent and winced. She couldn't believe how much Joedii had changed in only a couple days. Large chunks of her hair had fallen out, and the hand with the burn had withered and continued to ooze blood. She'd gone skeletal thin from fluid loss and her breathing was labored. Dafnii knelt next to the cot and took Joedii's hand.

"Dafnii?" Joedii opened her eyes with an effort.

"I'm here, Joedii." She gently squeezed Joedii's hand.

"Tell them…" Joedii was wracked with coughs and clutched at Dafnii's hand. "Tell them to close the cavern. Don't…don't let anyone else in there."

"But your discoveries, all your work!" Dafnii protested, but her spirit wasn't in it.

"You were right, Dafnii. This place is cursed. Don't let anyone else go down there. Bury this place and forget it." Joedii coughed again and then leaned over the side of her cot, vomiting blood into a bucket. "Just promise me," she gasped, "that you'll bury me here with it."

"I will, Joedii." Dafnii clutched her hand, overwhelmed by the senseless tragedy. "I will."

* * *

Everyone who attended agreed that sunset had been a fitting time for the ceremony. Joedii's shrouded remains were buried in a trench over a hundred meters away from the building but many refused to even get that close to it. The surviving excavators had advocated rigging the entire place with explosives and turning it into a collective cairn. Fortunately a lack of both time and explosives had made that proposition impossible, so everyone had satisfied themselves with sealing the entrances with dirt and hoping that was good enough until a more permanent solution could be made.

"It was a very beautiful ceremony," Dafnii said. "Short, but you would have appreciated that. You were never big on ceremonies. It wasn't denominational but we had…so many of you to bury." Dafnii gazed across the line of over fifty graves they'd dug in the desert; she was one of the few survivors from that fateful day when Joedii had first opened the canister.

"I wasn't sure what to leave for a marker, so I copied what I translated from the other markers around. I even translated it into the few modern languages I know. Maybe the next group of archaeologists will actually listen."Dafnii stood and brushed the sand off her trousers. She took one last look at the blocky structure in the distance and turned in the growing twilight, back towards the remaining lights of camp.

***

This is not a place of honor...no highly esteemed deed is commemorated here...nothing valued is here.

What is here is dangerous and repulsive to us. This message is a warning about danger.

The danger is still present, in your time, as it was in ours.

The danger is to the body, and it can kill.

The form of danger is an emanation of energy.

The danger is unleashed only if you substantially disturb this place physically. This place is best left shunned and uninhabited.

Let's Rob a Bank

In Aelelea, a city between worlds, six impossible things happen before breakfast.

Two people waited in a coffee shop. The other patrons of this shop, served by the clockwork-powered automaton staff, did not notice these two people. People go unnoticed all the time in coffee shops all across the multiverse, even more so in Aelelea where octopuses walk the streets when the twin moons raise the tide and hope is burned every night because it's cheaper than candles. But the woman in an emerald green dress with gossamer butterfly wings sprouting from her back gets noticed.

Or I should say even *they* get noticed. They are one of the Learned, a human who has achieved the apex of magical knowledge, who has become something simultaneously more and less human. A great many of the Learned prefer gender-neutral pronouns since things like gender begin to look increasingly irrelevant when you can manipulate fundamental forces of the universe. But it also means if a Learned is not interested in not being noticed by the general public, they *stay* unnoticed.

But I digress. The name of this particular winged person in the green dress was Anise, and they looked up from their cup of green tea and scanned the coffee shop for what felt like the dozenth time. "He did say he'd meet us here, right?" they asked as they tapped their nails against the bone china cup. Their companion merely gave a grunt of assent and did not look up from their work. A clockwork automaton lay spread-eagled on a black velvet cloth in front of the Cunning Artificer and they continued to make adjustments to the gears. "It's going on ten past two," Anise said.

"He'll wait until fifteen minutes after because he knows I'll leave if he hasn't shown up by then. Ah, there we go." The Cunning Artificer finished an adjustment and closed the automaton's casing. Its gears began ticking to life and the automaton sprang to its feet, gave a smart salute to the Artificer, and then jumped down from the table to join the rest of the coffee shop staff. The Artificer started putting their tools away in a brown leather case on the chair beside them. "The Jade Duke knows I'm a creature of habit and he exploits that to his benefit."

Where Anise was guaranteed to draw attention wherever they went if they so desired it, the Cunning Artificer seemed to purposely blend into the background. Their brown canvas coveralls and tweed flat cap was identical to the hundreds of mechanics, artificers, and engineers who built and maintained the wondrous infrastructure of Aelelea. But anybody who looked directly into the Artificer's steel-gray eyes knew there was something otherworldly about them. Those eyes looked right through you, measured, analyzed, calculated; after they concluded their inspection you always felt like you didn't quite measure up. Most people avoided eye contact as a result.

"Have you worked with the Jade Duke before?" Anise asked.

"Once or twice. Enough to learn his habits." The Artificer

finished putting their tools away and snapped the case shut with a click. They picked up their iced tea and took a sip. The Artificer never touched warm drinks, the Artificer did not believe in warm drinks. "Ah, Teal, I didn't realize you were joining us."

The Teal Witch slid into an empty chair next to the Artificer and picked up a menu. Witches are three a tuppence in Aelelea, but the Teal Witch was the only one who could call themselves Learned. Their hat was a subtle shade of their eponymous color, but their patchwork skirt and hand-knit sweater made them look like any of the dozens of witches who sold potions on this very street. "Sorry, got distracted on the way over, there was a sale on powdered fish feet and I've been running low. Has the Duke shown up yet?"

The Artificer took out their pocket watch and consulted it. "Three minutes he'll walk through the door and we won't be able to miss him." They angrily wound the watch before returning it to one of their pockets. The artificer drained the last of their iced tea and typed in the request for a refill at the order console in the center of the table. "Teal, do you want anything?"

"Pistachio muffin and green tea," they said not looking up from the menu.

The Artificer punched in their requests as well and leaned back in their chair, an eye on the front door. "I may have to actually get up and act as if I'm going to leave for him to show his face. Oh speak of the devil."

Every head in the coffee shop, including those of the mechanical staff, turned to look at the Duke when he came through the door. While the rest of the Learned went to efforts to *not* be noticed, the Jade Duke *enjoyed* using magic to make people pay attention to him. As always he was dressed in the finest of dandy style. He wore a three-piece suit of dove gray, complete with matching gloves, and a cravat of rich emerald with a golden tie pin. His black boots were contrasted with hunter green spats fastened with gold buttons. Completing his outfit was a top hat and overcoat of matching pale jade green.

He paused in the doorway, taking his time to languidly remove his hat and gloves as his eyes scanned the room, making everyone feel like he had seen them personally watching him. Most people, somewhat embarrassed, turned down their gazes and returned to their drinks. The Artificer, however, refused to look away and bored into the Duke with the impatience of someone who knew their time was being deliberately wasted. The Duke, however, had long grown immune to such petty concerns as the irritation of the Cunning Artificer.

"Dear friends, how glad I am to see that you're still here! I was unavoidably detained." he said, spreading his arms wide as he sauntered across the shop towards their table. An unoccupied chair shot out from the table and the Duke almost dropped his hat as he reached out to stop it. Out of the corner of their eye Anise had seen Teal make a magic gesture before the chair had suddenly moved and now there was a small, fierce grin on their face as the Duke readjusted himself.

"This isn't a social call, Gracey, and we both know it," Teal said as the Duke sat down. "You have business for us or not?"

"As a matter of fact I do." The Duke was momentarily jostled as a clockwork server brought a tray with two cups of tea, one warm one cold, and a pistachio muffin to the table. Anise swore she saw the Artificer wink at the automaton before it scuttled to another table. "Someone assassinated the Opal Dragon."

"We know that!" Anise said, feeling like they had to say

something to stay relevant to the conversation. "The city's been unable to talk about anything else for a week!" The Opal Dragon, another member of the Learned, had been one of the major players in Aelelea before their death. The city was still adjusting to the power vacuum which it had created and not even the Learned were sure how things would end up.

"Yes, but they've finally figured out what was stolen from the Dragon's house that night as well. The Dragon's personal directory has gone missing."

There were sharp intakes of breath from both Teal and the Artificer while Anise merely looked between the Learned, confused. "I don't understand, what's so special about this directory?"

"You, my dear Anise, are far too young to know this." The Duke turned to face them and smiled, propping his chin on his hands. "You have only recently joined the illustrious ranks of our Learned siblings. The Opal Dragon's directory was chock full of information which only she…"

"They," both Teal and the Artificer corrected automatically.

"They," the Duke continued, unperturbed, "which only they were privy to. Including the true names of our two companions here. Sadly, or perhaps fortunately for you, you had not yet come to the attention of the late great Dragon so your name is not among those loose in the world."

"Am I correct in concluding, Gracey, that there is a motive in you bringing us this information aside from the goodness of your heart?" Teal asked.

The Duke turned back towards them and smiled. "I don't know who stole the book initially, but I know the Fang Street Devils have it now. *And* I know where they're keeping it, *and* that it's going up for auction a fortnight hence."

"And anything you can do to screw over the Devils after that job in Camhurst," the Artificer finished. For a brief moment the Duke's facade broke, his eyes flaring with anger at the mention of the Camhurst incident. However the Duke recovered his composure and smoothed his moustaches.

"Yes. They know all manner of people would want to get their hands on that book if they could avoid paying for it, so the Devils have it locked up in the main vault of the Grand Avenue Bank."

"So, a bank job then." Teal looked over the rim of their teacup. "You get to teach your rivals a lesson and we," they pointed to themselves and the Artificer, "get to keep our names out of hostile hands. But what do they get out of this?" Teal nodded towards Anise.

"The job needs four people and we need to do it tonight. She was the only one I could get on short notice."

"You said the auction wasn't for another fortnight!" Teal protested.

"Yes, but the auction's being announced tomorrow and then everyone and their brother will be watching the Grand Avenue Bank. Not only will they double security on the bank, but anybody who did manage to walk out with the book will have to fight off every major player in Aelelea."

"Job would go better with five," the Artificer said. "Five's an even number."

"No it isn't," the Duke said, confused. "Are you going on about your weird number obsession again?"

"They mean it's more auspicious magically," Teal said. "We may be able to do the job with four people, but it would be better to do it with five."

"Job would go better with five," the Artificer repeated. "We could get the Bee Doctor or the Prismatic Bard. Their names are in the Dragon's book as well."

"I already asked and they said they wouldn't work with me," the Duke said. "Unless you can pull somebody out of thin air in the next five minutes, we're going to have to do this job with four."

A silent look passed between Teal and the Artificer; the two seemed to have some sort of conversation with only the barest of facial expressions. Eventually the Artificer grunted and downed the rest of their iced tea. "All right, we'll help you with this job," they said.

"But you're paying both of us as well. A hundred crowns each," Teal added.

"What? That's outrageous! You should be paying me for the privilege of going on this job."

"You already gave away the most important part for free," Teal said. "You need me to bypass the magical wards in the bank and you need Arty here to bypass the mechanical wards. I assume Anise here has some special talent."

"Illusions," Anise answered. "I'm really quite good at them."

"Interesting. But the point is we don't need *you* to do this. We could get our own team together to hit the Grand Avenue Bank. Or we could watch with everyone else. Or we could even participate in the auction if we were so inclined. We have all manner of options before us, but since no other Learned in the city will speak with you, you don't have such a luxury." The Artificer merely gave a grunt of assent.

The Duke waited, twirling his mustaches in apparent thought as he considered Teal's argument. "And the girl?" he asked.

"If you mean Anise," Teal said. "*They* are free to make whatever deal they like with you, however I would advise *them* not to do this job for free either."

Finding themselves thrust onto the spot Anise stumbled over their words before squeaking out. "A hundred crowns I guess?"

The Duke shot out of his chair and stormed around the coffee shop, muttering a great number of dark curses in a variety of tongues. The other patrons of the shop looked up from their conversations, stared at the sputtering dandy, and then ignored the public drama. "All right, fine," the Duke said as he angrily sat back down in his chair. "A hundred crowns for each of you. I hope you all understand I don't carry that kind of money on me, it'll have to be after we finish this."

"That's fine," Teal said. "I think we can trust you that far."

The Artificer counted out a few silver coins and dropped them into a slot in the center of the table's console. A light switched from red to green, signifying the bill had been paid. "All right," they said, standing up and picking up their tool kit. "Let's go rob a bank."

* * *

The streets of Aelelea were teeming with people at this time of day. Day shift workers were either heading home or out to enjoy well-earned time off with friends and family. Night workers just waking up for the day heading out for their "morning" coffee or tea and a bite to eat before going to sweep streets, bake bread, or harvest moonlight. The Learned walked through the streets with the efficiency of people used to the wonders of the city between worlds. But every now and then, Anise couldn't help but stop to look at something new to their still inexperienced eyes. No matter the hour the gears of Aelelea continued to turn.

Golems, ranging from simple gingerbread-man looking constructions to lifelike works of art, walked through the streets with the scrape of fired pottery. Fairies in a riot of colors navigated the air above, avoiding the trudge of the ground-bound crowds. Clockwork automatons ranging from two to ten feet tall stomped by on their metal feet, and everywhere you looked humans in every shape and size, humans from a thousand different worlds, each one having the potential to become the next Learned.

Anise's attention had drifted again when they bumped into the back of Teal. Their party had stopped in one of the many plazas of Aelelea, this one centered around St. Eligius's Clock tower. This tower commemorated the work of the countless mechanics and artisans who had labored to build this marvelous city. It was rumored that the Artificer had been there when the cornerstone was laid and had written a name on it in grease pencil before the next stone sealed it away forever. The tower's great bronze bell tolled three times to mark the hour. The Artificer pulled out their own pocket watch and consulted it. "Three minutes late," they said. "I shall have to see about getting the clock re-calibrated."

"Your watch could be running fast," the Duke countered.

The Artificer looked directly at him. "Three minutes late," they said again, returning their own watch to their pocket while keeping eye contact. "And Grand Avenue doesn't close until five. Do you propose we walk in and take it or wait until everyone's gone home for the night?"

"Just walk in and take it? Are you crazy?"

"We've both been accused of that, yes," Teal said.

"Some of us, not to exalt ourselves unduly, have a hard-earned reputation for probity and honesty," the Artificer said.

"The benefit of which is that very occasionally we can commit the most egregious of crimes and we are beyond suspicion."

The Duke once again looked flabbergasted. Anise suspected this was something that happened to him often but he didn't like to admit it. "You just admit to committing crimes in the middle of the street and nobody bats an eye!"

"You started this little expedition," Teal interjected. "I assume you have a plan?"

"The rough outline of one. Our new friend Anise, here, happens to be excellent with illusions. So we go into the bank now, while they're still open, and find a good place to hide. Have Anise cast an illusion over us so nobody can find us before they close for the night, and *then* we hit the vault. Or did that have too much subtlety for both of you?"

"It lacks a certain dramatic appeal," the Artificer said. "I was thinking we could have automatons tear the bank apart brick by brick until we found what we were looking for." By their tone it was obvious they were just trying to get a rise out of the Duke but he didn't take the bait.

"Or we could send an unkindness of ravens into the bank," Teal offered. "They're incredibly clever."

"And incredibly noticeable, gods preserve us." The Duke started down Grand Avenue, jade overcoat flapping behind him. "Come on, we're going with my plan." Anise saw the Artificer toss a coin to Teal who deftly caught it out of the air as the lot of them followed after the Duke. Grand Avenue was a broad tree-lined street with a double-tracked streetcar line running down the center. Carriages and wagons made their way along the flat paving stones, some pulled by flesh and blood animals, some by beings of clockwork, and some propelled entirely by magic. Anise almost lost track of the other Learned multiple times as they wove through the dense traffic.

The Grand Avenue Bank was a massive structure which dominated one corner of the intersection of Grand Avenue and Cedar Street, another of Aelelea's main thoroughfares. Like so many banks across the multiverse it had been constructed to imitate the temples of antiquity. The ground floor was in a pharaonic style with two massive sandstone pylons on either side of the bank's entrance, both decorated in elaborate bas reliefs showing people engaged in presumably some allegory about commerce. Rising above the pylons were the five stone tiers of the office pagoda, where the lords of finance looked down on the city they thought belonged to them. Flanking the stairs leading to the bank's doors were two massive bronze lions, currently at rest on granite plinths but actively watching everyone who entered and departed from the bank.

The Duke spent about a minute looking at the lions, pulling on his moustaches in thought. Rolling their eyes in exasperation the Artificer strode confidently onto the staircase between the two. The Duke sputtered in shock and dismay when both lions abruptly turned their heads to look at the Artificer with predatory intensity and then….remained on their plinths as their attention was drawn to other members of the crowd.

The Artificer looked back at them and waved. "Come on, we haven't got all day." Teal laughed and followed, skipping up the steps to join the Artificer. Anise looked at the Duke, who still seemed to be in shock, and then followed the other two Learned. As they climbed the stairs the bronze lions paid them no more attention than any of the other people going about presumably legitimate business. From the top steps the Learned looked down at the Duke, who was still standing nervously at the base of the stairs.

Eventually the Duke managed to screw up his courage and took his first step onto the marble staircase. Immediately both lions snapped to attention and looked directly at the Duke, who shrank into his greatcoat and looked ready to flee in terror as the lions both got ready to pounce. But then the Artificer whistled and the lions, docile as kittens, returned to their at rest positions. The Duke looked up at the Artificer with indignation. "You didn't think to mention this ability before?"

"Who do you think built them? And if you hadn't spent so much time skulking about with a guilty conscience they wouldn't have noticed you anyway. They're only programmed to notice people acting furtively, which even you should know is the best way to draw attention to yourself. Come on." The Artificer turned and opened one of the great brass doors of the bank and Teal and Anise followed behind them. The Duke hurried up the stairs and managed to slip through the door before it quietly thudded shut.

The interior of the bank had the oppressive hushed atmosphere often found in places of worship, corporate offices, and other locations with perhaps an overinflated sense of importance. This was at least partly because of the obscene amount of marble on the floors and walls which would make any sound reverberate like the best bathroom song session. Gilt gas chandeliers suffused everything in warm light and queues of customers were waiting to speak with tellers behind the ironwork counter. The bank would have preferred something more ornamental than iron, but to prevent the tellers from accepting fairy-glamoured counterfeits iron was absolutely essential.

The Duke strode past all of these people, projecting the

calm, confident aura that he was *meant* to be here, and headed towards the area of the bank dedicated to the offices of various clerks and accountants who did the tedious work of running the bank. The other Learned followed in his wake, ignored due to the sheer presence which the Duke was able to project, although Anise suspected that both Teal and the Artificer could make themselves go utterly unnoticed even without the Duke as a distraction. The quartet stopped at an unremarkable door with the brass plaque "Records Room" where the Duke pulled a key from his pocket, quickly unlocked the door and gestured for everyone to follow him inside.

The room felt incredibly cramped due to the presence of dozens of wood filing cabinets crammed against all four walls. The drawers were labeled in meticulous copperplate handwriting detailing their contents, and the center of the room was taken up by a reading table with half a dozen chairs around it. "And just why do you have a key to the records room of the Grand Avenue Bank?" Teal asked, crossing their arms as the Duke locked the door behind them.

"Research. Finding out who is in debt to whom has been well worth the initial investment in getting a duplicate of the key made. It was surprisingly cheap as well, almost every junior clerk has a key to this room and they're not paid terribly much. Anise, be a dear and glamour this room so nobody will notice us, will you?"

Anise closed their eyes and concentrated, folding their hands in front of their chest. Soon a lattice of green light surrounded them, spreading through the room and tracing over every object. The other Learned could feel the tingle of magic as Anise wove the green light into a blanket. "Rather well done," Teal said, inspecting the lights which were already fading in intensity. "I've never seen Yeats's Cloak applied over such a large area. Who did you learn that from?"

"I uh, sort of figured it out on my own," Anise said sheepishly as the light became an afterimage and then faded to nothingness. "It seemed like the most reasonable way to expand an illusion over a large area. Did I do it right?"

Teal looked at them in astonishment. "You figured this out by *yourself*? I know so-called masters of the eight disciplines who can't weave an illusion half as subtle as this. Duke, where have you been hiding this person?"

"In a back pocket for an occasion such as this," the Duke said smugly, drawing papers from an inner pocket of his greatcoat. "Now, if you're quite finished looking at Anise's handiwork, we've got a robbery to plan." He spread the papers out across the table and revealed a detailed building plan of the bank as everyone took seats around the table. "Based on my intelligence, the Dragon's book isn't in the main vault but instead in this side vault here." The Duke pointed to a small chamber located to one side of the main corridor. "This is set aside for some of the bank's customers who want to have discrete storage for valuable items that might attract unwanted attention from the law. The first barrier will be a set of illusions that disguise the entrance which I'm certain Anise will be able to handle with impunity, but it's not the only defense."

The Duke pointed to a small note written in magical runes next to the passage. "The next barrier is a series of hexes which I'm told the Opal Dragon put down themselves for a rather considerable fee from the bank. Teal, do you think you're up to the task?"

"Possibly, they got overconfident as the years went by so there's probably an exploit I can use. But I can't say without seeing it for myself. Besides, I thought hexwork was your bread and butter, I'm more of a generalist."

"Yes, but you actually studied under the Dragon, you're familiar with their work, there's a good chance there's something you'll recognize that I would just miss." Anise saw Teal look at the Duke, really *look* for the first time and their electric blue eyes bored into him as deeply as the Artificer's gray eyes analyzed the group. There was a moment where Teal looked like they were about to say something, but the Artificer gently touched their arm. Another unspoken conversation went between the two before Teal sat back, saying nothing.

"After Teal takes down the hexwork that just leaves the vault door. Arty, I assume you'll be able to handle that?"

"I have my tools," was all the answer the Artificer saw fit to give.

"Then we shouldn't have any problem. A couple hours after the bank closes we'll be in and out. Easy as pie."

* * *

Anise caught themselves nodding off again and pinched themselves to stay awake. The cup of tea had been several long hours in the past and had worn off entirely. It probably wouldn't have been so bad if they had something to do, but they were still waiting. There had been some brief excitement when a clerk entered the room with an armful of file folders and everyone held their breath as he put them in their proper drawers. Anise's illusion, it seemed, had worked perfectly because the clerk did not raise his head even once despite walking within six inches of the Duke. Everyone had let out a sigh of relief when the door clicked closed behind him.

Sometime afterwards the Artificer had rummaged in their tool bag until they'd pulled out a pack of playing cards. The cards were not a typical pack of playing cards with the familiar suits of cups, coins, clubs, and swords. In fact, Anise couldn't identify any suits whatsoever. The Artificer and Teal had started playing a game, but they had not offered to include either Anise or the Duke, and if there were rules to this game it was impossible for Anise to decipher them. They seemed to have just finished a round of the game when the Duke stood up abruptly.

"All right, it's seven o'clock. There shouldn't be a soul in the building, let's get going." Teal and the Artificer hastily put their game away and joined Anise and the Duke at the door. The Duke put his ear to the wood and listened before cautiously opening the door and peering outside. Satisfied that the hallway was clear, he gestured for the rest to follow him.

When open, the bank at least had the susurrus of hushed business transactions to take the edge off of the oppressive silence. Closed, Anise couldn't escape the feeling that they Did Not Belong Here that seemed to emanate from every wall of the bank. They flinched as their shoes clicked on the marble floor, wondering how everyone else passed without a sound. Maybe some sort of magic?

Pulling another ring of keys from his pocket, the Duke unlocked the staff entrance, which lead behind the great ironwork counter that separated the bank's tellers from its customers. Surprisingly, for a bank with its reputation, the tellers had not done a proper job closing, too eager to leave once quitting time came. One cash drawer had a set of keys still in its lock so that anyone could raid the contents. A few other cash drawers were cracked just a handful of inches which meant those tellers hadn't even bothered to lock up for the night. Ledgers and deposit slips were scattered all across the counter instead of being neatly organized and tallied for the day. But the Learned passed up all of this petty cash, available for the taking; they were after more valuable loot this night.

The staircase down into the vaults was just as impressive as the rest of the bank, more marble steps with railings of polished brass. The stairs had been enchanted to keep the stone from wearing down from the passage of thousands of feet over the soft marble so it remained as shiny and solid as the day it was installed. An enveloping darkness greeted them at the bottom of the stairs, so Teal snapped their fingers and summoned a sphere of pleasant yellow light to banish the darkness. Both Anise and the Duke started in surprise as a squadron of gleaming, eight-foot tall automatons were revealed.

"These weren't supposed to be here," the Duke said, eyeing the machines warily. "Automaton storage is deeper in the vault." The clockwork men appeared gilded, yet another ostentatious display of the bank's profits, but they were heavily built machines as well. Those great metal hands curled into fists at the automatons' sides would be capable of punching even a Learned into a fine paste.

"They're harmless," the Artificer said, walking forward with an easy confidence and giving the automatons no further thought. Teal followed in their wake. "They bank uses them to transfer gold and other precious metals around. They look scary but they're only capable of lifting and carrying." Hesitantly the Duke and Anise followed, but the metal machines remained immobile and unresponsive.

Overhead the vault's barrel ceiling was decorated with

mosaics depicting more idealized concepts of Commerce, Industry, Thrift, Punctuality, Probity, Proper Arithmetic, and a host of other virtues which bankers found worthy of admiration. There was a rumor that one mosaic was supposed to represent Compound Interest but Anise had no idea what it could look like.

"All right, Anise m'girl." (Both Teal and the Artificer hissed "THEY") "Have a look 'round and see if you can find that illusion hiding the vault we're looking for." The Duke consulted his blueprint and then pointed to a bit of wall which looked just like all the other bits of wall. "Should be somewhere about here."

Anise took a deep breath and looked at the wall, really *looked*. The thing about humans, fairies, and even octopuses is that none of us really see *everything*. Our eyes are only able to look at a certain amount of things at once and our brain just fills in with details. The key to illusion magic is to encourage the brain to fill in more details than it does normally. People, after all, often see what they expect to see. Sometimes an illusion can be defeated just be looking at it the right way, although illusionists are loathe to tell you this because it would undermine the mystique of their craft.

When Anise looked at the wall it was difficult; they couldn't find the illusion at first. But as they carefully scanned back and forth, their eyes kept sliding over a certain spot, as if their attention was gently but firmly being pushed away. It took a few times to notice because it was a very subtly crafted illusion. Carefully, Anise kept their eyes unfocused, barely brushing against the edge of the illusion until they could get one hand on the hem of this particular magical shroud.

"Come on, Anise, we haven't got all night," the Duke said,

impatiently.

"I'm trying!" Anise said, picking at the enchantment. A good spellcaster always tied up the loose ends to keep the enchantment from unraveling. But if *Anise* could *make* a loose end, it would be simplicity itself to pull threads out until the entire thing faded like so much mist after sunrise.

"If you're in such a hurry, you can unravel it yourself," Teal said, and then they squinted again at the Duke. Teal scurried over to where the Artificer was busy inspecting the bank's automatons and there was a whispered conversation but Anise turned their attention back to the illusion. They dug their hand into the mesh of the enchantment, something they had to do entirely by touch, and started to *pull*. At first the magic refused to give way, stubbornly clinging to the wall, but as Anise tugged and pulled the magic started to shift. All of a sudden there was a sub-audible tear as the illusion collapsed, revealing a cross passage.

"They do good work," Teal said appreciatively. They and the Artificer were already waiting and both of them pushed past the Duke to take the lead down the passage.

"Excellent work, Anise," the Duke said, and he gave her an awkward pat on the shoulder. "I knew I could count on you." Even though the Duke's hands were gloved, there was something about his touch that made Anise deeply uncomfortable.

"Nothing to it," they said, and hurried to join the other Learned. Anise was still new to the world of diplomacy and power games that were almost second nature to the small community of Learned. Unfortunately great knowledge of the world's mysteries did not always bring great wisdom or skill with interpersonal relationships. Even Anise knew the Jade Duke had burned through any goodwill among the Learned and clearly Teal and the Artificer were aware of this as well.

About ten meters down the hallway Teal had stopped and was crouched near the floor, examining something that only they could see, their large witch hat sitting on the floor behind them. The Artificer had pulled an electric light from their tool bag and was shining it to help Teal see as they carefully chalked notations on the marble floor.

"Stay back," the Artificer advised as Anise and the Duke caught up. "Teal says it's a particularly nasty hex and they need time to think."

"Aziz, light!" Teal shouted. "My sphere can't cross the hex line and so I end up with my shadow over whatever I'm working on!" The Artificer redirected their own lamp which they had let stray when they had addressed Anise and the Duke. Teal continued to mutter to themself, making more indecipherable markings.

"How's it going?" the Duke asked, stepping forward to look over Teal's shoulder.

"Better if *your* shadow wasn't *also* blocking what I was working on," Teal said. "Go back and wait, I'll tell you when I know." The Duke looked a little miffed at this response and was about to say more before the Artificer intervened.

"I would leave Teal alone for now, Gracey. Wouldn't want you to accidentally set off a hex set by the Opal Dragon. It was the Opal Dragon who made this hex, wasn't it? I distinctly remember you saying that." Without another word the Duke backed off, pulling at his mustaches in irritation.

Anise didn't know how much time passed as they waited and Teal muttered to themselves about the dynamic flow of energies and modifications of standard hexes. Eventually Teal stood up and put their oversized hat back on their head. "Did you do it?" the Duke asked impatiently. He stopped himself before stepping past Teal, realizing at the last moment he didn't want to set off any still-active traps.

"Yes, I disabled it," Teal said. "Although I'm not sure why you needed me to help. It had the Vermilion Drake's fingerprints all over it. They're competent enough but they're nowhere near the level of the Opal Dragon."

"Never mind that," the Duke said, striding down the hallway. "Come on, Arty, we've got a safe to crack."

"I really don't like it when you call me that," the Artificer said. They put the light back in their tool bag and followed the Duke. After another ten meters the hallway ended in a large steel door with a large wheel in the center of it. The Duke was already standing at the door, impatiently twisting the wheel without any real hope of opening it. The Artificer ignored both the Duke and the door and examined the steel wall the door was set into. "Should be somewhere around here…Ah, there we go." The Artificer pointed to a small brass plate affixed to the wall discreetly below eye level next to the door.

In proud but restrained letters the plaque said *Product of the Tubbs Safe Company, 19 Crochet Street, Aelelea.* The Artificer scoffed when they read that. "Really? Tubbs? They must have spent all their money on the illusion and the hex because they sure didn't invest the money when it came to the vault door."

"So you can get us in?" The Duke's eyes jumping between the Artificer, Teal, and Anise nervously. As if this close to success he expected everything to suddenly go sideways.

"In my sleep, probably. As a matter of fact, *you* could probably break it. Which leaves me wondering—"

"Listen, we don't have all night, just open the goddamn door."

Without another word the Artificer walked up to the door

and placed their hand upon it. They closed their eyes and there were small lines of copper light that radiated out from their hand before disappearing into the steel. In a matter of seconds everyone heard the clunk of the bolts sliding back and the Artificer took a grip on the wheel, pulling the door open on silent, perfectly oiled hinges. Without so much as a thank you the Duke ran through the door, leaving the rest of the party to catch up.

The inside of this vault was dedicated entirely to safe deposit boxes. The middle of the vault did not have a large, tempting pile of currency but instead a rosewood table where patrons could inspect the contents of their deposit boxes with the discretion of the Grand Avenue Bank guaranteed. The Duke was already attacking a deposit box, number 2777, with a pocket-sized crowbar he had pulled from somewhere beneath his greatcoat. All subtlety or patience was now gone and he gave a cry of exultation when the lock gave way with a metallic snap. He pulled the safe deposit box from the wall and tossed it onto the table with a thud, and threw open the lid to reveal a small, black, leather-bound notebook inside.

The Duke was about to grab the notebook but Teal slapped his hand away. "It could still have one of the Dragon's hexes still on it." Teal muttered some sort of incantation and waved their hand over the book. There was a dramatic pause followed by nothing happening, but in a very dramatic fashion. Everyone let out breaths they did not realize they had been holding. "All right, I *think* it's safe," Teal said and the Duke wasted no more time in snatching the notebook from the box. He opened it and his eyes sparkled with glee as he quickly thumbed through the pages.

"This is the Dragon's all right. I really must thank all of you for helping me, but unfortunately for you—"

"This is the part where you betray us," the Artificer said in a very tired voice as they drew a pistol from their tool bag. "By the gods, Gracey, you're so tediously predictable. You can't let even *one* job go off without screwing somebody over." Teal had also summoned an electric blue ball of flame that was dancing above their hands, ready to be unleashed.

"Well, it would seem you have me two to one and it would be foolish of me to try and fight both of you. But then, there are *four* of us aren't there." Teal and the Artificer both looked at Anise and for once their coordination faltered because they both shifted their aim to Anise. This was exactly the opening the Duke needed as he ran out of the vault with lightning speed. The Artificer snapped their pistol around and managed to get off five shots, but their aim was not true and the Duke escaped unscathed.

The Artificer was closest to the door and started after him, but only got as far as the vault entrance. "Everybody down!" the Artificer yelled, diving to one side of the steel door frame and curling into a ball. Teal created a half-dome of blue energy which sealed them in as tight as a bug under a glass. Anise had barely enough time to dive underneath the heavy table before they heard the loud roar of an explosion followed by the sound of stone falling upon stone. Anise pulled themselves even further under the table, not daring to look out.

"It's all right, Anise, you can come out, now." Teal was looking under the table and offered a hand to help Anise back to their feet as they crawled out from cover. Aside from a coating of white stone dust everywhere, the vault itself was remarkably unscathed. Teal looked into Anise's eyes, checking to see if they were concussed. "How are you feeling?"

"I'm all right," Anise said. "Mostly bruised feelings. Why did you two think I was in league with the Jade Duke?"

Teal at least had the decency to look a little embarrassed by Anise's question. "It's because you're new among the Learned. The Duke is so consistent in his treachery that nobody works with him more than once if they can help it. We didn't know if he was betraying you now or he had plans to betray you later in his little scheme. That's why Arty wanted to get a third person on our side to help stack the odds in our favor. I apologize for assuming you were in cahoots for when he betrayed us."

"But if he's such a consistently bad person to work with, why help him at all?"

"That damned book," the Artificer said, brushing dust off of their coveralls with very little effect. "It still has our past names in it and the Opal Dragon used those as leverage against us. We want that book destroyed." Anise nodded with understanding. The most dangerous threat to a Learned was their past name being used to bind them to another's will. Anise had spent a considerable amount of time erasing all record of any name connected to them that *wasn't* Anise. "He used a blast spell, by the way, Teal. Whole ceiling came down."

"But does that mean he isn't—"

"No, he is. I saw him pull a spell sphere from his pocket. *Might* have been an Okiro & Sons? I'd have to examine the fragments." The Artificer opened their tool bag again and pulled out a tiny clockwork automaton, maybe six inches in height. The automaton consisted of two little arms, two little legs, and one round, brass body that looked very much like a pocket watch. The Artificer inserted a key and wound up the little creature, which opened one big eye and came to life when it started ticking. The Artificer placed the machine on the table and leaned down to address it.

"All right, little guy, we're trapped behind a pile of rubble and we need you to—NO! Hey! Look at me! Look at me!" The automaton had started to wander off and was gazing at Anise with…it felt wrong to say longing but that was the only word that felt accurate. "Yes, they're very pretty but we need to rescue them as well as Teal and myself, okay? If we don't get out of here the police will find us and you'll have to break me out of jail. Again." The automaton nodded slowly. The Artificer extended a hand, palm up, and the automaton climbed onto it.

They walked out of the vault and towards the pile of rubble now blocking the only way out of the vault. Anise could see a gap near the very top of the pile, far too thin for any human to get through but perhaps large enough for the Artificer's automaton. The Artificer climbed as far as they could onto the rubble pile and placed their clockwork companion down. "All right, we need you to get to the other side of this rubble pile. You go down this hallway, take a left, and then you wake up your big brothers and have them dig us out. Do you understand that?" The little machine nodded. "Okay, repeat that back to me. No. Don't take that attitude with me, repeat it back to me."

The clockwork companion kicked a pebble and then began a complicated series of gestures with its tiny hands. Whatever it communicated with the Artificer they seemed satisfied. "All right. Be careful, don't get hurt." The machine scrambled up the mound like a billy goat and soon disappeared through the gap. "We should be out of here in no time. Teal, are you still able to track Gracey down?"

Teal rummaged through their pockets and pulled out a ball of string, a stone with a hole in the center, and a handful of other odds and ends. They began pulling the string in something akin to a cat's cradle, but far more magical looking with the inclusion of things found in a witch's pockets. "Yep, I can get a precise fix on him anywhere in the city, and I doubt he'll be leaving Aelelea."

"All right then, Anise, let's go over what your talents are."

* * *

A man stood at a street corner in the late night darkness, purposely avoiding the circle of light cast by a streetlamp. Despite the hour the street was not deserted because Aelelea never truly slept. Plenty of fairies, more accustomed to doing their work at night, were busy spreading dreams or encouraging plants to grow. Traders in moonlight, stored in great copper kettles, moved their stock when it couldn't be spoiled in the light of the sun. And of course, acts less than legal have been carried out at night since time immemorial and Aelelea was no exception.

The Duke had stopped by a safe house, really little more than a garret apartment, and had exchanged his trademark green ensemble for the clothes of a down-at-the-heels businessman who was engaging in a bit of that clandestine business. As nervous as he was, it took the Duke far longer to noticed the equally shabby looking businessman waiting across the street than it should have. On the surface there was nothing terribly remarkable about the man but there was something about how the Duke couldn't get a good look, as if his eyes kept sliding over...

The coin dropped for the Duke and in his shock he made a rookie mistake, he turned on his heel and started walking briskly for a dark alley.

He cursed himself as he did it, there was no better way to alerting a tail you were on to them than suddenly bolting like a startled animal. Stupid! Still, he couldn't go back now so his best option was to give this tail, whoever it was, a merry chase and try to lose them. It would mean delaying his rendezvous but that could always be rescheduled. But who could it have been who was following him? Nobody else knew about the Dragon's book yet, and he'd left Anise, the Artificer, and Teal buried under three tons of rock. There was no way they could have gotten out.

The Duke turned off the main street into an alley that was littered with crates, waste bins, and the other detritus that tends to accumulate in even the best-run cities. He was already shrugging off his overcoat when he ran nose-first into an invisible wall. The Duke let out a small yelp of pain and slowly, carefully reached out a hand. About where he'd been so rudely stopped his hand felt the roughness of a brick wall, despite his eyes telling him there was very clearly an alley extending all the way to the next main street.

The Duke could feel himself breaking out into a sweat; they couldn't have *known* he'd pick this alley, could they? Reaching out with both hands the Duke felt upwards. About half a meter above his head was the reassuring flatness of the top of the wall. If he got a running start he could probably make it over, and put this wall between himself and whoever was pursuing him. That was the key: don't panic, look for advantages and exploit them.

The Duke turned around and saw the ordinary man standing in the middle of the alley's mouth. "Ah, so terribly sorry, seem to have gotten turned around," the Duke blustered. "Hope you have a good evening, sir." The Duke tipped his hat and tried to push back the man but he continued to block the Duke's escape. Then the illusion melted away to reveal an extremely angry Anise. "

Anise!" the Duke said, putting as much false warmth as he could muster into his voice. "You made it out! Did they do anything to you? I was so worried about you!"

"Worried, huh?" Anise kneed the Duke in the groin and he doubled over in pain.

"All right, maybe I could have handled it better," the Duke said. "But you've displayed an incredible level of skill and intuition. How would you like to join me as my partner?"

"Oh, I don't think I could do that," Anise said. "You see, I've already got a prior commitment and unlike you I don't walk out on a deal. Oh, here comes one now." There was the merry ring of a streetcar bell and it soon came into sight trundling down the main thoroughfare. The streetcar didn't stop but a figure in brown coveralls with a distinctive brown leather tool bag stepped down from the car.

The Artificer looked up at the Duke, they were not a tall person but their gray eyes bored into the Duke and there was nothing at all friendly about their smile. "You know, we got to thinking and there were a lot of things that just didn't add up about this job. Like asking me to come along. Any halfway competent locksmith could get through a Tubbs lock and they come far cheaper than I do. So what was the *real* reason you needed me? But then, you knew Teal wouldn't do the job alone."

"But why would you need me?" Teal asked rhetorically. The Duke whirled to see Teal slowly descending from a rooftop next to the alley. Strands of blue magic swirled around Teal's feet, keeping them aloft. "The Vermilion Drake is good, but they're not *that* good. Even *you* could undo the Drake's hexes. And there's no way you didn't know any of this before hand. You had the bank's own building plans. So you bring Anise for the illusions, a locksmith for the vault, and you handle the hexes. Why bring Arty or I into it at all? Unless someone—at a guess the Opal Dragon themself—capped you."

The Duke chuckled nervously. "You really think you've figured it out? Well I hate to disabuse people of their false conceptions but—"

"Save it," the Artificer said. "I'm sure you have more spell spheres but they *are* expensive. And do you *really* want to have to use more than necessary when every Learned you've double-crossed discovers you can't do so much as a cantrip?"

"Listen, we can share, all right?" The Duke dug through his pockets until he drew out the Dragon's black notebook. "We'll use the book together, we'll be partners for real. Arty, Teal, I know the rest of the Learned don't give you proper respect. Anise, you can skip the politics all together and go straight to the top. We'll reshape this city, together we can— AAAAAAHHHH!" This last scream was the moment when the Duke realized the notebook had caught aflame in his hands due to a well-placed fire spell from Teal. He dropped it to the ground and tried stomping out the fire with his leather boots but to no avail as the book disintegrated into ash.

Teal landed behind the Duke and he turned on them. "You idiot! Do you have any idea how many secrets were in that book?"

"Oh, Gracey, of course we did," Teal said chidingly. "That's why we had the Opal Dragon killed."

There was a full moment as the enormity of what Teal had just said sunk into the Duke's head. "What, you mean you and…Arty?"

"I asked you to stop calling me that, you don't have those privileges," the Artificer said.

"Yes, the two of us," Teal said. "The Dragon had gathered too much power, they really needed to be stopped. So we hired the Fang Street Devils to do the job. Taking a Learned down isn't hard if you know their secret and in the time I spent with the Dragon I learned oh so many interesting facts about what you can do with a sprig of mistletoe when three full moons happen on a Tuesday."

"And you!" the Duke turned to the Artificer.

"Gave them the information to bypass the Dragon's defenses. It wasn't hard. We didn't anticipate the Devils trying to double-cross us but we shall soon instruct them of their error."

"Why tell me this?" the Duke asked. "I could turn both of you in to the authorities, unless, oh gods you're planning on killing me aren't you?"

"No, Gracey, we're not planning on doing anything as gauche as killing you," Teal said.

"Tempting though that option is," the Artificer added.

"Hush, you." Teal smiled indulgently at them before turning back to the Duke. "No, Gracey, we're condemning you to a life with the knowledge that at any moment Arty or Anise or I could let every single person you've betrayed, every gang you've double-crossed, every mark you've ever bamboozled know that you're powerless now. I'd try finding an honest occupation and staying the hell out of our way from now on if I were you. Come on, Arty, I could use some tea." With that, Teal walked past the Duke, now a shrunken shell of what he once was, without even so much as a look back.

The Artificer opened their tool case and rummaged around

until they drew out a wad of banknotes. They counted off a hundred and twenty crowns and pressed it into Anise's hand. "For your trouble, young Anise. I doubt he ever meant to pay us but I honor my debts." With nothing more they picked up their case and followed after Teal.

The Duke looked up at Anise, eyes pleading and desperate. "Please, Anise. You can't leave me alone. My magic may be gone but I still know things! We might not be able to rule the city, but we could stake out our claim while the Learned are still fighting. Please, I *need* you, Anise."

"For once," Anise said, "I think you may be telling the truth. I don't doubt that you need me, but I seriously doubt that I need you." Anise turned, not listening to the Duke's protestations behind her, and followed after Teal and the Artificer. They really did know some good tea shops.

In a couple hours, the sun would rise on the city of Aelelea and it would be breakfast time. People would open their papers to see six impossible things had already happened. The Grand Avenue Bank had been robbed, a cure for the Rusting Death had been found, the Fang Street Devils had descended into factions over some internal squabble, nobody had died at the Goblin Embassy ball, a third moon had been sighted in the skies over Aelelea, and the Jade Duke had disappeared without a trace. And life in the city between worlds went on.

The Ugly Duckling

Once upon a time there was an ugly duckling. What's that? You say you've read this story before? Perhaps you have and perhaps you haven't, but until you read to the end you won't know for certain, now will you?

Now, as I said before I was interrupted, there was an ugly duckling and he was born to a family of ducks who had lived in a flock of ducks for generations and all these ducks lived in a great big pond that was rather pleasant and nothing worse than a minor inconvenience ever happened to anyone. Now ducks are gossipy creatures, this is in their nature, and inevitably one of their favorite topics was the poor ugly duckling. "What a strange duck the ugly duckling is!" one of the ducks exclaimed. "I feel so sorry for his parents. Look at the way he swims, it's not like a duck at all!"

"And those feathers!" another duck added. "Not a single speck of yellow on them! What an utterly hideous shade of gray."

"And the way he eats! Just one thing at a time rather than mixing them all up," a third duck said. "Is that any way to behave I ask you?"

"Quite honestly I feel sorry for the parents," the first duck said. "Imagine being burdened with a child like that."

Of course this gossip got back to the ugly duckling's parents, as it always does in any tight-knit community of ducks. They could not help but take it somewhat personally. After all, this was *their* child everyone was talking about. It reflected badly on them as parents to have such an odd, ugly duck. So they decided Something Must Be Done and spoke with their wayward child.

"You don't swim right," Father Duck said. "All that flailing about with your legs. Good ducks don't swim like that."

"I *like* swimming this way," the ugly duckling said. "It just feels right to me."

"But it's not right!" his father said. "You need to swim like a duck. Can you promise me to swim the *right* way?"

"Yes, Papa."

"And the way you eat, it attracts notice," Mother Duck said.

"What's wrong with the way I eat?" the ugly duckling asked.

"You pick at your food, dear," his mother explained. "A good duck doesn't worry about what he's eating, he just *eats*."

"But I like the unique flavors, I like tasting them one at a time."

"It's not *right*, though. Can you at least try eating like a *normal* duck?"

"Yes, Mama."

"It's a shame we can't do anything about your feathers," his father said, looking the ugly duckling over. "White we could work with, but gray." The ugly duckling hunched down, acutely conscious of his feathers now. "Just try to stay in the back, maybe nobody will notice."

"Yes, Papa."

His parents tried to get the ugly duckling to act more like a duck and the poor little ugly duckling tried. He really did. But everything he did always seemed to be not quite right. He tried to quack like a duck but his quacks were just never quite the right sort of quack. He tried to walk like a duck, but his waddle was never the right sort of waddle and his feet were black instead of orange besides. He tried to swim like a duck, but it was never with the same grace and agility of his duck siblings. The ugly duckling became very sad because despite his best efforts he just was not a very good duck.

The other ducklings were not kind either. I wish I could say we lived in a world where children were kind and cruelty was only something that came with the cynicism of bitterness and old age. Unfortunately we are not blessed to live in such a world. Every day the other ducklings would peck at him, reminding him that he *was* an ugly duckling and an odd one as well. No other duckling found enough compassion in their heart to befriend the ugly duckling and he grew up very lonely indeed.

Time passed, as is the way of the world, and the ugly duckling grew up. What's that? And he grew into a beautiful swan? No, he grew into an ugly duck. His feathers did not come in the iridescent green and blue of a proud male duck. Nor did they come in the dun brown of a respectable female duck. They were white! Nothing but snowy white feathers from his orange bill to his black feet. (Which, I might add stubbornly remained black and never became orange.)

And the ugly duck was *large* as well. Much, much larger than his duck siblings who all grew to respectable duck sizes.

"I wish you didn't eat so much," his mother said. "Look at the size of you! No self-respecting hen will want to go out with such a large duck!" The ugly duck tried to make himself smaller, but with very little success.

"We should have done something about your feathers," his

father said. "They didn't come in right at all. Maybe next season."

"But I *like* my feathers," the ugly duck protested, although truth be told his heart wasn't much in it. He felt ashamed that his feathers weren't the right color, as if it was his fault they came in white instead of green.

"Well, there's no two ways about it," his father said. "You've been dealt a bad wing, you'll just have to try to be the best duck you can despite your disabilities."

And the ugly duck did try. But once again, his swimming was not like the other ducks and any time he tried to copy them it ended up an exercise in frustration. He always landed flat on his face instead of gracefully gliding like a leaf upon the pond. And his quack never came out right, sounding too much like a loud, undignified hoot. Sad to say, many other ducks mocked how he quacked, saying they couldn't understand him with that thick accent. So the ugly duck spent quite a lot of time alone so he could be himself without worrying how he looked to the other ducks.

* * *

One sunny day, as the ugly duck was idly swimming in circles in a deserted part of the pond he heard someone say, "My, what a beautiful swan!" (No, I was not being deceitful earlier in our tale. The ugly duck did not grow into a swan because he had never *known* what a swan was. Being a duck was the only thing he'd known his entire life, and everyone told him he was a very ugly duck.) The ugly duck looked around, confused, trying to find who was speaking.

A sparrow flitted down onto a branch that leaned out over

the pond and looked at the ugly duck. The duck had some experience with sparrows. They had never been cruel and mocking like the other ducks so he did not mind their company, and sparrows always knew where the tastiest seeds were around the pond. "Hello, were you the one who spoke right now?"

"Yes, I was," said the sparrow. "I meant what I said, you're very beautiful."

"Who, me?" The ugly duck shrunk, trying to make himself smaller. "No, I'm just a duck. And a rather ugly one as well."

"Nonsense! I've traveled quite a great distance in my short life and I've seen plenty of ducks and plenty of swans."

"I've never even heard of a swan," the ugly duckling said. "What are they like?"

"What are they like?! Oh, how to put it in words. Ducks are fine folk, don't get me wrong, but swans are so much *more*. Their feathers are always the purest white, like newly fallen snow. When they call, their regal trumpets echo across the pond and creatures everywhere fall silent in respect. You may not be a duck, but you are a very beautiful swan."

"I am?" the swan asked.

"Of that you can be certain," the sparrow said. "I'm sorry to talk and run, but I heard there's a very nice collection of seeds and I simply must fly. I just wanted to say good day." And with no further comment the sparrow flew off.

The swan took a moment to look at his reflection in the water, really *look*. The swan had never spent much time looking at himself. Every time he did was just a reminder of how different from all the other ducks he was. It was natural he'd avoid trying to look at himself. But the longer he looked, the more he became convinced. How could he possibly be a duck with that great long neck of his? Or his snowy white feathers? Or his great, wide wings? He didn't know exactly what a swan was, but surely that was a label that fit him better than duck. He was so excited that he swam back home immediately to tell his parents.

* * *

I wish I could tell you that his parents were overjoyed to have a swan for son. That they welcomed him home, embraced him, and introduced him to all the other ducks as their child, the swan. In a just and proper world such a thing would be the natural course of events, as rivers flow towards the sea and as the sun rises in the east. But as you and I know, we do not live in a just and proper world.

* * *

"Don't be ridiculous!" his father said. "I'm a duck, your mother's a duck, all your grandparents were ducks, we've been ducks for forever!"

"But you have to admit that I'm not a very good duck," the swan said.

"That may be so, but we didn't have any of this swan nonsense when I was a duckling," Father Duck continued. "Where are you getting such strange ideas from anyway?"

"I spoke with a sparrow…"

"Sparrows! And pray what might they know about ducks? I think this sparrow just made this swan nonsense up on the spot."

"Are you sure you're not just doing this for attention, dear?"

Mother Duck asked. "I will admit, you haven't had an easy life as an ugly duck but wouldn't it be better for you to try to fit in? Instead of drawing attention to how different you are?"

"But what's *wrong* with me being different? What's so wrong about being a swan?"

"I just don't think the other ducks are going to accept some made-up nonsense about you being a swan. Wouldn't you rather just be a duck?"

The swan was starting to get discouraged. He didn't know a lot about being a swan, he had only found out today after all, but *surely* he wasn't a duck. He tried again. "But I'm not *happy* as a duck. Don't you want to see me happy?"

"*Of course* we want to see you happy," Mother Duck said. "But is this really the right thing? It might just be a phase for all we know."

"Calling yourself a swan won't help you fit in with the other ducks. You just need to act more like a duck," Father Duck said. "Forget about all this swan nonsense."

"Yes, Papa," the swan said. Although he did not intend to forget about it in the least.

* * *

The very next day the swan swam up to a group of ducks who were busy gossiping and tried to introduce himself. "Hello!" he said. "I just found out I'm a swan!"

"Oh really?" one of the ducks said. "And what does that mean?"

"Well, I suppose it means I'm not a duck. I only found out swans existed yesterday."

"And just like that you think you're a swan?" Another duck

said. "I think you're a little confused. You grew up with us, we know you're a duck."

"But I'm different from you," the swan said. "Surely you've noticed."

"Yes, bad enough to be different," a third duck said. "But do you really have to shove it in our faces?"

"I never cared about you being different," a fourth added. "But now you're just drawing attention to it."

"I think you're just delusional," the second duck said, preening his feathers. "You're a duck that *thinks* you're a swan. You can't just *become* a swan."

"He raises a good point," the first duck said.

"But I am!" the swan protested.

"Listen, you want to live with this absurd fantasy that you're a swan, that's fine," the second duck said. "But that doesn't mean *I* have to participate in it. You're an ugly, odd duck and you always have been."

"Yeah, you have a lot of audacity dragging us into this," the third duck said. "We're not freaks like you."

"But I…" the ugly duck tried to respond.

"Don't bother," the fourth duck interrupted. "Let's go get something to eat." And with that the four ducks swam off, irritated that the ugly duck had bothered them.

The ugly duck tried to talk to some of the other ducks, to make them understand *why* he thought he was a swan. But the ducks were not sympathetic to his arguments, no matter how eloquently he worded them. Eventually some ducks grew violent towards the ugly duck because he persisted in his absurd delusion. And his parents, who saw the fuss that he had raised, became more distant from their ugly duck offspring. The poor ugly duck, who really, truly was a swan, found himself more isolated than ever. Some time afterwards the swan died of a broken heart and the ducks were quietly glad the drama of the ugly duck had come to an end.

* * *

A cygnet, like any baby creature, is not ugly. Just because it doesn't walk like a duck, or quack like a duck, or swim like a duck does not mean that it is an ugly duck. Maybe it's a duck that ducks differently than other ducks. Or maybe it's a swan that doesn't know it. If we don't give it the chance to grow and become itself, how will it ever know? In a just and proper world all children would grow to become who they know they are on the inside and their parents would celebrate.

We do not live in a just and proper world, but that does not relieve us of the duty to make it one.

A Murder at Wyndingham Manor

Thomas Cahill, sixth Baron of Wyndingham woke as he had for the past forty-eight years at precisely six o'clock and rose to perform his morning toilette. When he reached for the water tap he found despite his best efforts he was unable to turn it. "Damnation, taps have rusted shut again. If it's not one thing it's another. I've half a mind to just hand the house over to Richard and retire to a cottage down in Kingsport." Cahill emerged from the bathroom, smoothing out his beard. "I swear if one more thing goes wrong with this house I…Oh."

It was at this point Cahill realized he was dead. He may have risen at his usual hour but his body, stabbed through the heart with a bayonet, had remained pinned to the bed. "Well that's damn inconvenient." Realizing you're dead is never a pleasant experience and it was understandable that Cahill had to take some time to come to terms with the fact. Which is probably why he didn't hear his maid come into the room until she screamed and dropped the breakfast tray.

"The Baron's dead!"

"Yes, you think I can't see that you silly woman? You don't need to drop the breakfast all over the floor."

"There's been a murder! The Baron's been murdered! Someone call the police!" The maid ran out of the room in hysterics, breakfast completely forgotten.

"Alice!" Cahill ran after her. "Alice, get back here and pick up the breakfast at least! You damn, damn silly woman." This was only the beginning of Cahill's morning of frustrations as all the servants, from the butler all the way down to the hall boy, came into his bedroom to confirm the Baron was extremely dead. But Cahill could at least understand the desire of his family servants wanting to pay last respects to their employer. The indignity he could not stand was the arrival of the police who, of course, tramped mud all over the carpets in their hobnailed boots as they scoured the scene of the crime.

"Well, he's definitely been murdered." said a detective-sergeant as he jotted in a notebook. "And they's done him in with a bayonet."

"Here now, sergeant, surely that's a dagger?" asked a constable.

"Naaaah, that's a sword bayonet, that is!" The sergeant put one hand on Cahill's chest and pulled the bayonet out with the other.

"Do you mind, sir?" Cahill asked. "You're getting blood all over the sheets!"

The sergeant continued, unaware of Cahill's concerns. "Recognize it from my time in the Army. They only issue these to the Rifles. Here, Jack, you gather the male servants up and see if any of 'em served in the Rifles. I bet we find our killer that way."

"It won't do you any good," Cahill said. "I know every servant in the house and I can guarantee not a single one of them served in the army, much less the Rifles. Listen, if you'd just telegraph my wife she could probably help." Despite his best efforts Cahill remained unheeded and when the police finally finished interrogating every male servant who could have done a stint in the army they were just as perplexed as before. The initial report had little to say other than "Baron Wyndingham murdered by person or persons unknown."

By that evening nearly all of Cahill's immediate family had arrived at the estate. Richard, his eldest son, was the first to arrive, coming directly from his railway office in the city. His wife Margaret arrived next with her spinster sister Alexandra, and his daughter Regina brought with her a tide of relations and friends who wished to give their condolences at this time. But of his younger son, Victor, there was no sign.

The next day they held the funeral in the village church, prayers offered up to the deities and a sacrifice made before the sacred grove, done in the proper fashion. Cahill appreciated the effort his survivors put in but it all seemed so dreadfully banal, lacking in any true emotion. It would have been nice to know that his relatives felt *something* after he passed aside from some mild annoyance. Only Regina, always a truly sensitive child, wept openly during the funeral. Richard, as was his wont, was all polite efficiency as he handled the million and one details that must be seen to after the death of a parent. He seemed to take solace in having work to do. Margaret walked through everything in an emotional fog, clearly shocked that such a violent event could have happened in her own home.

Three days after the funeral, the family solicitor, Aloysius Montgomery, arrived to present Cahill's last will and testament. The family, including the incorporeal and invisible Cahill, gathered in the parlor to read the will. As Montgomery unsealed the document at a writing desk Victor dramatically entered the house."Ah, mamá, dear brother and sister, I hope you shall forgive my tardiness!" he said, removing his coat with a flourish.

"Of course, Victor makes an appearance when it's time to talk about money," Richard grumbled. "Spent all your allowance at the gaming tables again?"

"If you must know, dear brother, I was unavoidably detained by a storm during the crossing and could only arrive just this minute. Someone really must do something about the Western Railway and their utterly inadequate time tables."

Richard flushed at the jab. "*Great* Western Railway."

"Adequate Western Railway would be more accurate." Victor said as he pulled off his yellow gloves. "*And* I had to travel second-class, the absolute shame of it…"

"Victor, stop antagonizing your brother." Margaret interrupted. "By all the gods, child, your father is dead. Have you no sense of dignity?"

"Only what I learned from you, mother dearest. I imbibed it with my milk. Well, whatever Richard left behind."

"Victor you go too far!" Richard jumped from his seat. "I ought to thrash you bloody for your insolence."

"Children, please!" Margaret's patience had clearly run out. "I'll have the stable hands horsewhip both of you if you don't stop it this instant."

The brothers ceased their bickering but the family knew from long experience that this was a temporary armistice in the feud. Richard returned to his seat and Victor leaned rakishly against the piano.

"Right, if that's everyone I'll go ahead and open the will." Montgomery took out a paper knife and broke the blob of red sealing wax on the will. He unfolded it and began reading in a clear voice.

"I, Thomas Kendrick Cahill, sixth Baron of Wyndingham,

being of both sound mind and body as attested by my solicitors, do hereby make my last will and testament. In keeping with the laws and customs of the Regens Imperium my eldest son, Richard Sebastian Baldwin Cahill, shall inherit the title Baron of Wyndingham as well as the entailed property of Wyndingham Manor. A dower of one thousand pounds per annum, to be paid through interest on my portfolio of consols, shall be paid for the maintenance of my wife Margaret Anne Emerson-Cahill until her death, upon which event they shall revert to Richard. For my daughter Regina Eleanor Cahill a dowry of five thousand pounds has been established in trust, the interest of which shall be used for her maintenance until such time as she marries."

The family nodded at all these bequests, these were expected and Cahill had carefully outlined his plans to his family in the event of his death. What came next was a shock to everyone, Cahill included. "For my dissolute, feckless son Victor Graham Gavthorpe Cahill, I leave the entirety of one shilling, may he spend it wisely." Both Cahill and Victor jumped at that.

"Dissolute? Feckless? How dare you, sir, I'll have you know I am absolutely brimming with feck!"

"Feck, Victor, not fu-"

"Richard!"

"Honestly, mother, you know he doesn't read anything not to do with horse racing or forni-"

"That is *not* my will!" Cahill shouted but his family continued to argue heedless to his complaints. The analysis of his son Victor was accurate, but he certainly would never have put such a damning statement down to paper. And he distinctly remembered making a provision for Victor in his will. Albeit not a generous provision, but it was definitely greater than a solitary shilling.

"What on earth is going on here?" Cahill floated across the room and looked over Montgomery's shoulder to look at the will. The document *appeared* genuine, it had all the requisite signatures and seals but this document was clearly a forgery. Especially when Montgomery got to the next sentence.

"The remainder of my estate, including all stocks, bonds, and real estate holdings estimated at a value of fifty-thousand pounds I leave to my niece Hillary Catherine Forsythe."

"He did WHAT?" Richard and Victor shouted in unison, their fratricidal argument forgotten for the moment. Regina burst into tears again, overwhelmed by the emotional atmosphere, and her Aunt Alexandra took her into the garden for some air. Margaret kept her composure much better than her offspring but from many years of marriage Cahill could tell she was not weathering this revelation much better.

"Would you care to explain yourself, Mr. Montgomery?"

Montgomery looked at the will again, carefully examining the text of the document. "I'm sorry it's quite clear here on the document. The primary heir is Hillary Forsythe."

"That's not my will!" Cahill shouted, although as usual nobody noticed.

"This can't be his will," Margaret said. "He *detested* the Forsythes!"

"Oh well, Maggie, that's not really fair. Intensely *disliked*, yes, but I wouldn't go so far as detest."

"I assure you, Lady Wyndingham, I removed this document from the firm's safe this morning and I have every reason to believe it is accurate. We can check with the Court of Probate if you'd like but it'd take time. A week at least."

"That is not my father's will!" Richard protested. "I have *seen* his will before, I was named executor!"

"That's a good point," Cahill said. "That's not my will! Check my own safe! The combination…oh damn. Damn, damn, *damn*. Of all the bloody *stupid* things to go and do!" Cahill had been perhaps a bit *too* conscientious about keeping the combination of his safe secret.

"Good luck contesting that will in court, brother," Victor said wryly. "You know our Uncle Forsythe will fight for this tooth and nail. If that's everything I'll take my shilling and be off. I've tickets for the opera tonight."

"Victor, this is no time to be gallivanting off to your amusements!" Margaret said.

"Oh I assure you, mamá, this is far more entertaining than the opera. Richard is always a delight when he builds up a head of steam."

"Oh that is so typical of you," Regina said from her seat. "Get us all riled up and then leave so we have nobody to turn on but each other. I'm so sick of this entire family!" Regina got up and stormed towards the parlor door. "You all may fight however you want but I'm a woman grown and I am under no obligation to suffer in silence!"

"Regina, you come back here!" Cahill shouted and just as Regina was about to exit the parlor door slammed shut. Regina attempted to open the door and rattled the door handle aggressively but it remained immovable. Regina turned and glared at Victor.

"I suppose you think that's funny? Where'd you put the key, Victor?"

"I didn't do anything!" Victor had his hands up in surrender, backing away from the door.

"Victor, this had better not be one of your little pranks again,"

Margaret admonished.

"Mamá, I swear, I had nothing to do with this!"

"Victor!"

"Honest truth!"

The family descended into a cacophony of argument, everyone talking at cross purposes and nobody listening to each other. Cahill screamed in frustration, "Good gods, such a family I have been blessed with they can't even let me rest in peace!" Suddenly the will—the forgery—burst into flames and Montgomery shouted in surprise before dropping it into an ashtray. *That* was enough to get even the argumentative Cahills to stop.

Montgomery looked at the smoldering ashes of the will and then to the Cahills. "I think we may want to call in Mr. D'Quay."

* * *

The family had settled down, the door to the parlor finally opening when one of the chambermaids came to clean out the fireplace. Even Victor was paying attention. "Mr. D'Quay is a private investigator who has, on occasion, done work for our firm before. He is eminently discreet and comes recommended by the highest sources."

"Whom?" Margaret asked.

"I cannot say directly but let us say he has been of tremendous assistance in matters of state." The Cahills all looked suitably impressed. "More importantly I think we require the skills of his associate, the occult investigator Dr. Chelsea Dobson."

"Dr. Chelsea Dobson!" Regina's eyes lit with delight. "Oh mamá, we simply *must* invite them! I am dreadfully interested in her theories of lithomancy, there was an article in the Lady's

Home Gazette…"

"You would bring an occultist into our home? A confidence trickster?" Richard didn't bother to disguise his scorn. "I shan't have it. We live in an era of industry and science, not mumbling superstition."

"And yet," interjected Montgomery, "let us consider what we all witnessed here today: First the door the parlor slammed shut, despite no window being open allowing a breeze to disturb it. The door then proved impossible to open despite the best efforts of both Regina and Baron Wyndingham. Second the will of the former Baron, the subject of intense emotional disagreement among all of you, spontaneously combusted. As much as I hate to say it, we must consider the presence of the supernatural."

This was enough to mollify Richard, at least for the present. "I believe we shall be taking your recommendation, Mr. Montgomery," Margaret said. "Please wire Mr. D'Quay and Dr. Dobson immediately and ask them to come at their earliest convenience."

"But a private investigator?" Victor asked. "Should we really allow our private affairs to be brought under such scrutiny? To say nothing of the expense!"

"I will admit that Mr. D'Quay's fee is considerable," Montgomery conceded. "But I have enough evidence here to conclude there are irregularities with the late Baron's will and I believe that a fresh set of eyes may immediately notice what we have not. Obviously the police cannot be counted upon to bring the investigation into the former Baron's death to a satisfactory conclusion. Considering that a fortune in excess of fifty thousand pounds is at stake the fee of a private investigator would be well worth it. If D'Quay and Dobson can solve this murder we may find who altered the will."

* * *

D'Quay and Dobson arrived at Wyndingham Manor the next day. Victor had left the previous evening, making some vague excuse about prior commitments but the rest of the family was waiting to greet them when they arrived in the early afternoon. D'Quay walked with a blithe spirit, twirling his walking stick as he stepped down from the carriage and crossed the drive. "Good day! The family Cahill, I presume?" There was a nod of assent from the family members and D'Quay continued, "I am Jonathan D'Quay, private investigator, gladly at your service." He walked up and offered his hand to Richard.

"Richard Cahill, well, Baron Wyndingham now," Richard said as he shook D'Quay's hand. "This is my mother, Lady Wyndingham, and my sister Regina."

"A pleasure to meet you all, although under such unfortunate circumstances. You all have my deepest condolences." He kissed Margaret's and Regina's hands when offered and gave a sincerely charming smile. His smile faltered, however, when the deceased Thomas Cahill emerged from Wyndingham Manor to look over this private detective. Cahill got the distinct impression that D'Quay could actually see him, but then D'Quay was interrupted.

"Excuse me, Mr. D'Quay," Regina said. "But is your associate Dr. Dobson with you?"

"Ah yes, Dr. Dobson! You must excuse her, she has a large quantity of equipment that she always brings whenever we have to leave the capital. Dr. Dobson! One of your fans requires your attention!" D'Quay waved towards a woman who was overseeing the unloading of several crates from a railway freight wagon that had followed the carriage to the estate. From this distance what she was saying was inaudible but she appeared to be hectoring the unfortunate servants who had conscripted to help unloading.

"Give her a minute, she'll join us directly," D'Quay said. "Now your solicitor Mr. Montgomery explained very few details in the telegram and I read the obituary in the *Times* but I still have very little information to go on."

"D'Quay, you had better not be charming information out of our clients without me there!" Dr. Dobson had ceased harassing the servants and was coming towards the family with the energy of a battleship at flank speed. "It is absolutely vital that I receive all information to perform a proper scientific inquiry. It's bad enough the police have already been through here mucking everything up. Dr. Chelsea Dobson, at your service." This last sentence was directed towards the Cahills in a rather perfunctory manner. "Now, if we could please see the scene of the crime? We've already lost quite a lot of time."

"Please excuse my associate, too much lab work has affected her brain."

"If you would both follow us," Margaret said, intervening in what was clearly a well-worn argument between two friends. "We can take you to my husband's bedchamber." The party entered Wyndingham Manor and proceeded up the grand staircase towards the family chambers. Thomas followed, floating over his family like a trailed kite.

"The Wyndingham title dates back to the first Empire War, the first baron was a highly successful admiral raiding Amastican shipping during the conflict. He built the estate with his prize money and invested the rest..."

"This is all very fascinating, Lady Wyndingham, but if you'll pardon me saying the history of the estate may not be germane at this moment," Dr. Dobson interrupted.

Margaret accepted the point with good grace and changed tack. "There's not much to say. Thomas was found by Alice with a sword in his chest."

"Was an autopsy performed?"

"The inquest saw very little point, it was incredibly unlikely he had an apoplexy."

"Perhaps," Dobson said, but it was clear she was unsatisfied with the answer.

"Who all was in the house that night?" D'Quay asked.

"All of the servants were present, so far as we know," Margaret said. "Except for my lady's maid. She was with Regina and I. We were visiting my sister Alexandra."

"And all three of you can account for the presence of each other?"

"As much as anyone can."

Dobson and D'Quay exchanged a look. "And Lord Cahill, I'm sorry, Lord Wyndingham now. Where were you the night of the incident?"

"I spent the night at my club. There was a board meeting that ran rather late that day and I missed the last commuter train that evening."

"You could have ordered a special," D'Quay said

"It would have taken so long to get a locomotive under steam that I'd be better off taking a ride on a midnight freight."

"Couldn't you order an engine from somewhere else, I mean you're a vice president of the Great Western after all," Dobson asked.

Richard gave her a look of unabashed horror. "And interfere

with the operation of the railroad? It simply wouldn't do!"

Dobson hmmed thoughtfully at this but D'Quay made no comment. "And what of your younger son?" he asked.

"The gods alone know," Margaret said. "Victor comes, he goes, with nary an explanation. The servants didn't see him but that doesn't mean he wasn't here. You don't suppose Victor could have done it, do you?"

"We can't exclude the possibility," Dobson said. "But we're still collecting data so there are a great many things which are possible."

"The police said there was something special about the knife used to kill father," Regina said.

"Sword bayonet from the Rifles, fat lot of good that clue did them," Cahill said.

"I'm sorry, what was that?" D'Quay asked.

"The murder weapon," Regina said.

"Ah yes, I believe the police report said it was a sword bayonet. It could mean something."

"Or it could not," Dobson countered. "Was there any other evidence found in the room? Signs of entry? Footprints? Anything of that sort?"

"No, I'm afraid the police said wasn't much to go on," Richard answered. The party arrived at the late Baron Wyndingham's bedchamber and both D'Quay and Dobson went inside.

"Ah, excellent!" Dobson walked over to a crate that had been placed on the hearth rug and pried open the lid. "Excellent, excellent, I can begin work with my tools at once!" She bent into the crate and began removing devices that the Cahills could only hazard a guess at their purpose.

"Well, if you very kind people don't mind, we shall begin our investigation. I shall examine the room and try to find any clues that the police may have missed while Dr. Dobson shall attempt to commune with the spirit of the deceased Lord Wyndingham."

"It'll be a miracle if they actually notice me," Cahill grumbled.

"May I stay and watch? I'm ever so terribly interested in the spiritual sciences!" Regina asked.

"Absolutely not!" Dobson and D'Quay said in unison.

"What, haha, what we mean to say," D'Quay amended, "is that we are both involved in extremely precise tasks that require our absolute concentration. As much as we would appreciate an audience I fear that it would only be a distraction."

"Please, I've read the entirety of the Fox Sisters' literature on spiritual investigation, plus most of Margery's *Guide to the Spiritual Sciences*. Oh, what is that? Does it utilize electricity?" This last comment was directed towards a series of instruments that Dobson was retrieving from the shipping crate.

"It is extremely delicate and dangerous in untrained hands and no, I haven't the time to train you now," Dobson said. "Lady Cahill, please, there will be ample opportunity later but we must do our work first." With a little more cajoling from D'Quay the Cahills were finally shooed out of the bedroom and D'Quay closed and locked the door.

"Thank the gods, I thought they'd never leave. Especially that Regina." He pulled out a handkerchief and dabbed at his forehead. "I don't know why I let you keep talking me into these investigations. Sooner or later people are going to get suspicious."

"You're the one who has an entire reputation built around the idea that you're a brilliant detective who utilizes only inductive reasoning from physical evidence to solve crimes. And if they haven't noticed you *only* do murders yet they're not liable to catch on. Besides, I just got this equipment and I wanted to give it a field test." Dobson placed a collection of wires in a star shaped formation on the floor and hooked them to a battery. "Lord Wyndingham, if you'd be so kind as to step in the center of the pentacle, please."

"What is this infernal device supposed to do?" Cahill asked and then stopped. "You…you just spoke to me. Can you hear me?"

"Yes, we can both hear and see you," Dobson said. "I must say, you're rather well behaved for a ghost. Most of the ghosts we've run into there's been an awful lot of wailing and cursing, just unending ghastly noise. Maybe we should investigate for the gentry more regularly."

"I'm terribly sorry about this whole charade, when I saw you outside I nearly gave the game away then and there," D'Quay said. "Jonathan D'Quay, Dr. Chelsea Dobson, you've already met us so to speak. You are the late Thomas Cahill, Baron Wyndingham, yes?"

"Yes, I am."

"Excellent. Now if you could tell us everything about the night you were murdered so we can tell your relatives and the police."

"Just, tell you how I was murdered?"

"Honestly just the who is sufficient for our purposes even if it was an absolute stranger a rough description—and the fact that it *was* a stranger is enough to get us going in the right direction. How is helpful but even the police can usually figure that out. We did have one case where the victim was poisoned and *then* shot to cover up the poisoning as a misdirection but I would call that an outlier. I'm sorry, I'm getting distracted again."

"You're the great detective," Cahill said. "Shouldn't you be telling me how *I* was murdered?"

Dr. Dobson began laughing at this point and D'Quay gave her a pained expression. "Oh dear, you'd think this conversation would get easier every time I have it. Do you mind if I smoke?" D'Quay asked.

"Ordinarily yes, but I'm dead so it doesn't seem to matter terribly much."

D'Quay took out a cigarillo case and sat at Cahill's writing desk. "The honest truth is that I'm little more than a fraud. The famous detective act, it's all a facade. My true ability lies in being able to speak to ghosts like yourself. It's why I only do murders. Ghosts generally don't have much so with burglaries."

"Then why the act?"

D'Quay lit the cigarillo and smoked briefly before answering. "The most obvious reason is that Regenite law as it exists now does not recognize the existence of ghosts or testimony given by ghosts. It's all well and good for me to *say* that the ghost of the victim told me in precise detail how they were murdered, but no court in the entire Imperium is going to let a prosecutor use that as evidence."

"So we have to pretend that I'm actually a tremendously intelligent detective capable of figuring out an entire sequence of events from a handful of very small clues. Usually once the perpetrator is confronted with evidence of their crime they'll confess. If they don't want to the police can take it from there."

"What about Dr. Dobson? Are you really an occult investigator?"

"I am although with very little success."

"But you know ghosts exist! You can speak with them! I didn't even know ghosts were real until I became one!"

"Yes, but I can't *prove* it. All of my evidence is based upon my own perceptions and it is entirely possible my senses have been deceived. I had a great-aunt who was utterly convinced she was the Immortal Empress but that doesn't mean she *was*. Did live to be a hundred and six, though." Dobson stopped, chewing on the end of a pencil in thought before shaking her head and continuing. "Anyway, the important point is that aside from Jonathan, myself, and a handful of other people we know the majority of people cannot sense or perceive the presence of ghosts. My goal has been to find devices that would enable the larger human population to communicate with spirits of the deceased. So far my efforts have been fruitless."

"So that's why you've put a collection of wires and a lead-acid battery on the irreplaceable carpet in the middle of my bedroom?"

"It's an electric pentacle, I have a correspondent on the continent who swears it works but I have my doubts. Would you mind terribly stepping in the center?"

Cahill sighed and obligingly stepped inside the pentacle. "What happens now?"

Dr. Dobson connected the wires to the battery and there was a concerning hum as the current spread through the wires. "I have absolutely no idea but at this point I'm throwing absolutely everything at the wall at this point. Do you feel anything? Notice anything?"

"I'm sorry, I can't say that I do."

"Blast. I had rather hoped that electricity would prove to be the key to all this. There were all sorts of interesting phenomena when the first power plant opened five years ago. You may step outside the pentacle now."

Cahill attempted to leave the pentacle but a wall of blue light rose from the wires and shocked him. Cahill shouted in pain. "Was that supposed to happen?"

"Oh my gods, it works! It actually works! Could you try doing that again? Please, I need more data on this phenomenon."

Cahill gave a doubtful look at Dobson but D'Quay, standing behind her, encouraged him to try again. Cahill steeled himself and attempted to to pass through the pentacle again with the same results as his previous effort. "Absolutely fascinating!" Dobson jotted something down in her notebook and then approached the pentacle. "And yet physical flesh," she waved her arm across the barrier created by the electrified wires and nothing happened, "remains absolutely unimpeded! The first actual results I have had with an apparatus!"

"I don't suppose you could let me out now?" Cahill asked.

"Oh, yes, of course." Dobson broke the circuit and Cahill was once again able to drift freely through the room. "Although I wonder if you're capable of getting into the interior of the pentacle while the circuit is engaged. Lord Wyndingham, if you don't mind…"

"I think poor Lord Wyndingham has suffered enough of your experiments for today, Dr. Dobson." Dobson gave D'Quay a moue of discontent but he ignored it.

"Well I'm afraid I can't give you any information on who murdered me," Cahill said. "I was asleep when it happened."

"Well, that certainly complicates things."

* * *

"This is the problem with you gentry families, there's too much money involved and people can't wait for inheritance," D'Quay said. He, Dobson, and Cahill were out walking the gardens of the estate, ostensibly looking for clues but in reality covering for the fact D'Quay was at a loss on how to proceed.

"Let's try to look at this logically," Dobson said. "We need someone with the means to commit the murder, as well as motive and opportunity. The will benefits the Forsythes to the detriment of everyone else so the Forsythes are the most logical suspects."

"That's not my will, though," Cahill protested. "I've been very clear on that point even if you're the only two who have listened."

"I think your actions were enough to cast doubts upon the legitimacy of the will," Dobson said.

"My actions?"

"As Mr. Montgomery and your family explained, the forged will burst into flames when it was revealed to the family. Now I do not have a *large* body of evidence for this but what evidence there is suggests ghost can affect the material world if extraordinarily powerful emotions are involved. I believe it was your frustration and anger that caused the will to burst into flames. Fortunately Mr. Montgomery is perhaps a fellow traveler and was wise enough to call us into the case."

"So," Dobson continued, "as with most of these matters we need to ask the all-important questions: whom does this benefit? Let us first consider the Forsythes. Is it possible for the Forsythes to have planted the forgery and arranged the murder. Who are these Forsythes, exactly?"

"My much younger sister Catherine married Ronald Forsythe about twenty years ago. I was very much against it at the time and my experiences with him have only hardened my opinion against him. And it's not because he's a doctor, it's because he's an extraordinarily *bad* doctor in my opinion."

"Oh?" Dobson was intrigued by this statement.

"Yes. He runs an asylum out of Otterburn Bridge. I went to visit the asylum once and it was a truly barbaric place. People caged like animals, nothing more than heaps straw to sleep upon, some of them covered in their own filth. He has no interest in curing his patients, only keeping them from polluting society at large."

"Good gods, is this sort of thing legal?" D'Quay asked.

"Oh the state encourages it." Cahill's voice trembled with barely controlled outrage. "A good portion of his income is from state payments to maintain people found criminally insane and remanded into his custody. The state doesn't much care what happens to the criminal elements and Forsythe sees no reason to expend more than the absolute minimum on his charges."

"What about his daughter, Hillary? She's named as the beneficiary in your will. Would she have a motive for murder?" Dobson asked.

"Hillary? I find it exceedingly unlikely she'd commit murder, much less plan one. She's barely nineteen and in the years I've known her she's been....well..."

"Foolish? Silly? Inane? Banal?" D'Quay asked.

"Unremarkable. I don't want to be unkind but she's just sort of...there, if you get my meaning. I've never heard her express an opinion on anything and there are times I doubt she has the capability of forming one. Personally I blame Catherine. She treated her daughter as a doll and that's what she became."

"Well what about her parents then?" Dobson asked. "It seems possible they could try to control the fortune through their daughter."

"That I wouldn't put past them. Relations with Catherine have been strained ever since our father died. She thought she was entitled to a larger share of the inheritance but I thought with her husband supporting her and only her daughter to care for it made sense for her to get a third. She's never quite forgiven me for it and I could see her concocting a plan with Ronald to disinherit my children in favor of Hillary."

"Well that's certainly motive," Dobson said. "Let's put a pin in that for now and come back to the Forsythes. This is going to be unpleasant Lord Wyndingham, but we need to discuss your family. When money's involved even the bonds of family can become inconsequential. When it comes to your original will how was the money distributed?"

Cahill stopped and placed his hands behind his back, calling up the terms of his will in his mind. "The provisions for Regina and Margaret are identical in the forgery and in the will, that part is consistent. The chief difference is the distribution between Richard and Victor. I did not cut Victor off with only a shilling. I may disapprove of Victor's feckless lifestyle and failure to put his hand to anything redeeming but he is still my son. I left him around five thousand pounds in a trust. He'll have access to the interest but not the principal. The remainder I left to Richard to manage as he saw fit."

"Hmm," Dobson tapped her pencil against her chin in contemplation. "Well, let us analyze motive, then. Regina and Margaret I suspect we could rule out. There doesn't seem to be much benefit for them in committing a murder one way or the other. What about your sons? Are there any reasons they might desire to hurry along their inheritance?"

"I am not sure how Victor subsidizes his lifestyle but since he came of age he has never asked me for money. I can only assume he's more successful at gambling than he appears. As for Richard. Well."

"Yes?"

"Richard was always fiercely independent, determined to make his own way in the world. I must confess he and I have never seen eye to eye. I think that's why he went directly to the railway after he finished his exams at university. But he's done rather well for himself."

Dobson hmmed thoughtfully and chewed on the end of her pencil. D'Quay looked at her and groaned. "You have that psychological look in your eye again."

"Just because it's a new science doesn't mean that it's any less worthy of consideration than more established fields. Our own investigation into the occult is a new field."

"There's a world of difference between the two! At least we can actually see ghosts!"

"What are you two arguing about?" Cahill interrupted.

"Dobson's got her head all turned around by this latest school of thought about why people do the things that they do."

"At least it's trying to find a motive. Richard is a *fascinating* bundle of contradictions: a scion of aristocracy who rejects tradition and embraces the modern, even going so far as to take a job with a railway. Could there be a subconscious resentment of his father, representative of the old order which needs to be swept away for the new?"

"Good gods woman, do you hear yourself?" D'Quay rolled his eyes in exasperation. "Some people just hate their parents. You don't need to make a novel out of it."

"You're both ignoring the fact that Richard couldn't have committed the murder." Cahill said.

"Whyever not?" D'Quay asked.

"He missed the last train that night, he couldn't have come here to commit the murder."

"His denial about ordering a special train seemed rather odd to me," Dobson said. "I was curious about that."

"You have to understand, Richard holds very few things sacred in this world but a railway timetable is one of them. He would *never* interfere with the railroad's operation."

Dobson seemed dissatisfied with this response but she didn't push the matter further.

"What about the staff?" D'Quay asked. "How many people do you have employed on the estate?"

"We have twenty-six household staff who manage the house interior and around thirty groundskeeping staff, gardeners, gamekeepers and the like. That number fluctuates a little depending on the season but we're just shy of sixty or so."

"That's a rather large list of potential suspects. Could any of them have a motive?" D'Quay asked.

Cahill shrugged. "I can't say for certain. Walter, our butler, hadn't mentioned any issues among the staff but he could have decided it wasn't worthy of my attention and nobody's been dismissed recently."

"While it's not impossible for a staff member to have done this, I don't think it's likely," Dobson said. "I think the forgery is central to all of this. If we find the forger we find the murderer. I will say this would be a lot easier if we still had the forgery."

"Well I'm sorry, I didn't know I could make things spontaneously combust. I've never been dead before." There was a ring of a bell and the three looked up to see a telegraph messenger riding their bicycle up the drive of the house. "That's strange," Cahill said, "I can't imagine what that telegraph would be about."

"We'd better head back to the house, it may be from Montgomery's law firm," Dobson said and went from a casual walk to something not quite a run but faster than a brisk walk. Cahill easily managed to keep pace with Dobson while D'Quay struggled to keep up.

"Chelsea! Gods above and below, woman, why do you have to move so fast!"

They found Richard at the entrance of the estate, the envelope of the telegram ripped open and discarded on the ground. Richard looked like he was trying to set the telegram itself on fire with the power of his mind "What happened?" D'Quay asked, gasping for breath from his run up the drive. "What's the news?"

Wordlessly Richard handed the telegram over to D'Quay and stormed into the estate, loudly shouting for his mother and sister. The telegraph consisted of just a single sentence: Proposed to Hillary, she accepted. - Victor.

"Well, that certainly moves Victor to the top of my list of suspects," Dobson said.

* * *

"That bloody, misbegotten, feckless, miserable bastard brother of mine!" Richard was at full steam now and there was no solution but to let him vent the pressure. Fortunately this seemed to consist entirely of pacing back and forth and swearing incoherently. "That worthless fuc-"

"Richard!" Margaret was much accustomed to Richard's little explosions but she clearly drew the line at certain profane words. "There is no call to be so indecent about your own brother."

"He is after the family fortune, mother!" Regina said, just as angry as her brother and matching him in volume and intensity. "Name one thing, one solitary thing, Victor has done of value in his entire miserable life."

"You know perfectly well that I do not play favorites among my children." Regina and Richard both laughed at this.

"We're all adults, mother, there's no need to pretend," Regina said. "None of us have cared for Victor terribly much. As a child he would goad Richard and bully me, school only honed his natural inclination to provoke."

"Harsh but true," Cahill commented, watching his family argue with detached interest. D'Quay and Dobson nodded.

"Be that as it may," Margaret replied, "it is uncharitable for us to assume ill intent of Victor until proven otherwise."

"We absolutely must get the original copies of the will to prove the Forsythes are not the heirs," Richard said. "The representative from the safe company should be here the day after tomorrow."

"Why the delay?" Regina asked.

"I'm not sure, the company gave me a vague answer of prior commitments and insufficient staff to satisfy the request."

"Have you told your brother that you're going to open the safe?" Dobson asked, inserting herself into the conversation.

The Cahills looked up, having forgotten they weren't alone. "No, I haven't mentioned it to anyone. I only got a letter back today," Richard said. "Montgomery is still fighting with probate court to get the registered copy. And gods alone know how long that might take."

"If I may make a suggestion," Dobson said. "Why not send a telegram off to your brother that you're opening the safe? His reaction may be revealing."

"You're not seriously suggesting that Victor killed our father?" Regina was aghast at the suggestion. "He may be contemptible but not even Victor would stoop so low."

"It may not be Victor who did it," D'Quay said in an effort to calm the family. "But we can't discount the possibility, considering his sudden engagement to Hillary, that he may be connected."

"We're simply proposing that you leak information to Victor and see what happens next," Dobson continued. "Or rather, D'Quay and I shall investigate what happens next."

"Oh, that reminds me, have you made any progress in your spectral investigations?" Regina asked, all thoughts of Victor banished and excitement obvious in her eyes. Dobson and D'Quay both looked towards Cahill who was floating between the two of them.

"My research is ongoing," Dobson prevaricated. "There is some evidence of a spectral manifestation but I need to perform additional research."

"I'm right here!" Cahill said angrily. "Some evidence of spectral manifestation! Perhaps I should try burning the house down, maybe that would get people to take me seriously!" D'Quay looked distressed and nervously took out his cigarillo case, Dobson merely gave Cahill a look that could have killed if Cahill wasn't already dead.

"Dr. Dobson, are you all right?"

"Yes, Regina, just some spectral interference," Dobson answered as Cahill laughed. "I will make sure you get first view of my report when it's ready to publish."

* * *

"I don't like going behind my family's back like this. It feels incredibly dishonest."

"Lord Wyndingham, please, I am running on about four hours of sleep and you are doing nothing to improve my mood," Dobson whispered. Cahill, Dobson, and D'Quay were hiding across the hall from Cahill's study where his immense safe was located. Over Richard's protests D'Quay had sent a telegram to Victor informing him the safe would be opened soon. They had kept vigil the previous night with no result so if Victor and the Forsythes were to strike it had to be tonight.

There was a snore next to them and Dobson shook D'Quay awake. "I'm awake!" D'Quay mumbled, rubbing the sleep from his eyes. Wordlessly Dobson handed him a thermos of coffee. "Anything happen?" he asked as he unscrewed the lid.

"You fell asleep," Cahill said helpfully. "It was quite exciting."

D'Quay rolled his eyes in exasperation. "Anything *else*?"

"Not... Wait, everyone quiet." Dobson cupped a hand around her ear and strained to listen. Soon D'Quay and Cahill could also hear the steps of someone trying, unsuccessfully, to move silently through the house. "Not a word," she whispered and covered herself with the gray veil. D'Quay crawled back under the card table, disappearing beneath the tablecloth.

A circle of light appeared, going to and fro across the carpeted floor of the hallway and just as suddenly disappeared with a snap of metal. A floorboard creaked and a shadowy figure appeared in sight. Cahill could hear Dobson and D'Quay hold their breath as the figure crouched before the door. They attempted the doorknob and the unlocked door swung open easily. It wasn't locked, of course it wasn't locked, why would it have been? Everything of value was in the safe, there was no need for the door to be locked. The intruder stepped inside, snapping their dark lantern open again to navigate the study.

Cahill floated forwards but Dobson and D'Quay, waited for their prey to enter the study fully and become committed to their task, ensuring they would be unable to escape. The burglar had found the safe and placed a stethoscope to the safe's door, intently listening to the tumblers as they rotated the dial. Despite being dead, Cahill still needed light to see and the starlight was insufficient for him to make out the thief as little more than a black mass. He turned back to the room across the hall and waved.

As silent as Cahill himself, Dobson rose from the chair and advanced, her silhouette masked by the veil she had draped over her body. D'Quay was slightly more obvious in his approach but the burglar didn't notice, all their attention was focused on the task of opening the safe. They didn't even look up when D'Quay struck a match and turned on the gas lamp. "The window's locked and anyway it's a ten foot drop. You might not hurt yourself on the way out. Might."

"I ought to have known it was a trap, it was a little too obvious a challenge. But then I've come to expect a certain honest bluntness from Richard, not one for devious plans." Victor rose, removing the stethoscope from his ears, and turned to face them. "But then he didn't send the telegram, did he?"

"No," D'Quay said. "I must admit, forgetting to replace the copy of your father's will in his document safe was a considerable oversight on your part considering the amount of work replacing the will in the lawyer's office was."

"Not really. The Grovetown office of a major law firm is such a busy place, after all, so many comings and goings. Who's to notice one extra scrivener taking documents into the document vault? Although I think they'll find their files have been rather mixed up for some time. But yes, I failed to consider the safe here because I thought changing the lawyer's copy would be enough."

Dobson gave a mocking round of applause. "Quite the plan, Victor. It shows remarkable initiative. Based on your family's description I wouldn't have thought you capable. Although that does beg the question of why you went to all this effort."

"You were quite well taken care of, you know," D'Quay added. "You could have lived quite comfortably."

Victor gave a sardonic laugh. "Not with the debts I've accumulated. I've exhausted credit in every casino and gambling house on the continent. I've made pledges I can never hope to redeem. But there's a plan, see? I finally have a system, a guaranteed system, but I just need the cash to launch it. I can double the fortune, triple it! I just need the starter money to do it!"

"Do you really think the Forsythes would hand it over to you?" Dobson asked. "They'll sink that fortune into the hospital he's been struggling to keep open for all these years."

"Not if I marry Hillary first! If she's my wife anything that belongs to her legally becomes mine! We'll be wed this time tomorrow and my aunt and uncle will have no choice but to agree."

"And what does Hillary think of all this?"

"I honestly don't know nor do I care. She said yes, she's a means to an end. I can buy her off later or—well—accidents happen."

"You know, Victor, you disgust me," Dobson said. "And not just because you're a murderer, I find that distasteful enough. It's because you're so tediously *predictable*, you upper class twits all are. It's always down to money with you; even when it seems like there's some passion involved it's passion for money. You didn't even hate your father, did you? You just saw him as an obstacle to what you wanted that had to be removed. If it had been anyone else in the family, *maybe* some emotions might have been involved but you felt nothing."

"Shut up! It wasn't like that at all!" Victor was visibly distressed now. "You don't know anything about me!"

"You're going to resort to violence now because I've touched a nerve and you need to feel in control of the situation," Dobson said calmly. "By all means, take your weapon out. A knife, I assume? A pistol risks far too much noise if you're trying to be stealthy."

Victor fumbled at his waist and pulled out a dagger, brandishing it at both of them. "You stop that! Stop categorizing me! I'm not like Richard, I'm not some soulless automaton that only has room for timetables in his head! I'm living life!"

"Are you, though?" Dobson asked, clearly unconcerned by Victor's vehement threats. "Your brother is a sober, stolid, reliable individual. A fixed point which a lever to move the earth could be affixed to. So was your father. Is your rebellion really all that surprising? You fear the confines of that life so you throw yourself into the exact opposite: flighty, irresponsible, libertine. Your life is just as dictated by them as if you had followed in their footsteps."

"Shut up!" Victor's face flushed and he seemed to have stopped caring about the noise.

"Dobson, we may want to stop antagonizing the boy," D'Quay said worriedly.

"Oh there's nothing to worry about," Dobson said blithely. "That's why you murdered your father in his sleep, isn't it? You haven't the courage to face someone who could fight back."

If Dobson was going to continue this line of psychological inquiry she had no opportunity because Victor charged forward, slashing with his dagger. Dobson blocked with her left hand and got a nasty gash across her arm for the trouble. Dobson boxed Victor's ear with her right hand and Victor staggered, disoriented by the blow. D'Quay hurled an inkwell from the desk at Victor, splattering ink across his clothing and distracting him from his assault. With a roar Victor lunged at D'Quay, the dagger coming down and scraping across the desk's varnished surface.

D'Quay fumbled behind him, trying to find something, anything, to counterattack with. Reaching blindly, he grabbed a steel-nibbed pen and jabbed it point-first into Victor's thigh. Victor screamed in pain and collapsed as a sweeping kick from Dobson took Victor's feet from beneath him. Dobson stomped on Victor's wrist and he released the dagger with a moan and the crunch of fractured bones. Dobson bent down and retrieved the dagger. "Well, just goes to show…" D'Quay stopped when Dobson put the dagger against his jugular.

"Jonathan, I want you to think very long and very hard about the next words that come out of your mouth. Because if you spout a certain aphorism regarding pens and swords I will unfortunately have to write a long, extremely detailed letter to your sainted mother about how her youngest, most beloved son managed to get himself killed through his own stupidity. I may even weep as I write it."

D'Quay audibly gulped. "Goes to show that you can't even trust family in this day and age?" The last words were inflected as a question and D'Quay winced as Dobson took the dagger away from his neck.

"No, and what a shame that the world has come to this.

Damn, another shirt ruined." This last was directed towards her shirtsleeve which she seemed to have finally noticed. Dobson prodded the wound experimentally. "Flesh wound. May leave a scar but I won't need stitches. Cahill, did you keep brandy in this study of yours?"

"I had whiskey in the cabinet with the globe on top of it, I presume it's still there."

Dobson opened the cabinet and removed a glass bottle. "Ah, blue label, only the finest of quality here. Shame to waste it like this, though." She pulled the stopper out with her teeth and hissed as she poured it over her wound. Once it was clean she took a good fortifying dose for herself and handed the bottle to D'Quay. D'Quay helped himself to a rather larger helping from the bottle.

At that point Alice the chambermaid, who had been woken by the commotion, arrived at the study door and looked aghast at Victor lying prone and defenseless on the floor. D'Quay smiled at the poor woman, raising the whiskey in a toast. "Ah, help at last. Go wake the rest of the house, would you? And could you get someone to ring the police on the phone? It seems we've captured our murderer."

* * *

The three of them were back in the garden, enjoying the afternoon sun. By coincidence the locksmith *and* the copy of Cahill's will from the probate court arrived on the same day. The copy in the safe and the copy from probate were identical and reflected Cahill's original intents. The forgery found on Victor matched the scorched remains of Montgomery's copy. The Forsythes had been displeased at the loss of money but were quick to break ties with an admitted patricide.

"So what happens now?" Cahill asked. "Am I a ghost for forever or—what?"

"We don't know," D'Quay said. "The reasons why someone becomes a ghost are numerous but a great many fall into the category of unfinished business. If someone's been murdered the most important unfinished business is bringing their killer to justice. But that varies from person to person. I've seen ghosts move on once the killer is captured, others until a guilty verdict is reached, and some not until sentence is carried out."

Cahill made a face of disgust. "I can't say I'm very much interested in that last option."

"Nor can I blame you," D'Quay agreed. "But some ghosts just remain, continue going on being ghosts for reasons that Dobson and I have yet to discover."

"I will, though! Someday! I'm going to lick this problem yet!" Dobson mumbled. She had gotten far less sleep than D'Quay and had indulged rather heavily in medicinal whiskey, and so was suffering entertaining effects as a result. Cahill smiled indulgently.

D'Quay merely shook his head at his friend's inebriation. "But what happens next is entirely up to you, Lord Wyndingham. Follow your children, look after your wife, go haunt an opera house somewhere."

"Never did care much for opera."

"A castle on the moors, then, whatever you like. But you are by no means bound by Wyndingham Estate if you don't choose to be."

"S'true! Met a ghost up in the…the…the uplands. Up that way." Dobson pointed in a random direction and D'Quay mouthed "Up north" to Cahill. "S'frum tha Continent, waz doin' a…whatchum…sightlook."

"Sightseeing tour," D'Quay interjected tactfully. "Dobson are you sure you'd rather not lie down?"

"M absltly fine, yer worryin too much. Imma just sit down right…right." Dobson plopped rather ungracefully underneath an ash tree and fell asleep almost instantly.

"I'm not relishing the prospect of waking her up," D'Quay said. "But that's a later problem. Anyway, the point we were trying to make is you have an unparalleled level of freedom now that no living person can imagine."

"Yes, I suppose I do," Cahill said. "Shame it took dying to realize that."

A Matter of Protocol

When the rocket stands before us, like a tower of glass and steel
Then no words in any language can express the way we feel
Mingled joy and hope and terror as we're starting on our way
When we suddenly considered that it just might help to pray

The song came unbidden into his mind as he approached the landing craft. Chief Hughes had grown up in a religious colony on a small moon on the fringes of human expansion and most of the entertainment consisted of old Earth folk songs. You can take the boy out of the weird fringe colony but you can't take the weird fringe colony out of the boy he guessed. Although he probably would be whispering more than a few prayers before this mission was over.

He stepped onto the open boarding ramp of the craft and looked inside. The passenger compartment, with its two rows of crash chairs, was empty but an abandoned tablet was plugged into an outlet and running a diagnostic. Hughes stooped and picked up the tablet, scanning through the diagnostic results, and frowned. If they were going to launch on schedule somebody was going to have to spend time with a spanner readjusting the antigrav coils.

"So then I said to him, 'Well you know what they say: a girl without a dick is like an angel without wings.' And I sort of winked at him, right?"

"What'd he say to that?"

"Well he just kind of blushed and stammered a little bit. It was so fucking cute, so I cupped my hand under his chin and asked him, 'You ever fly with an angel before?'"

There was a loud laugh from the flight deck. Hughes looked up with the expression of a superior who has found people slacking off when there is work to be done—this is a universal look that transcends time and space. He unplugged the tablet and started up the short ladder to the flight deck, making as little noise as possible. The laughter cut off abruptly when his head became visible.

"Gutierrez. Ryu. I hope that we're doing pre-flight checklists while we're discussing our off duty adventures?" Neither of the women managed to meet his gaze and only Ryu managed a mumbled "Yes, Chief" in response. "What was that?" Hughes asked.

"Yes, Chief!" Ryu said, louder this time.

"Good." He thrust the tablet into Gutierrez's hands. "The antigrav coils need adjustment. See it gets done."

Gutierrez looked through the diagnostic and then up at Hughes. "Chief, these are well within standard tolerances. Do we really need to go dragging panels off to fix something that isn't broken in the first place?"

Chief Hughes looked her in the eye. "Those tolerances are written assuming nothing will go wrong. As a survivor of eight combat drops let me tell you right now, something *always* goes wrong. Fix it. If you can't do it yourself, find deck crew to do it for you. I know how popular you are among them." Gutierrez blushed at this last comment, an accomplishment between her lack of shame and deep brown skin.

Like most pilots in the fleet, Gutierrez had an ongoing antagonistic relationship with the deck crews. The deck crews worked hard every day to keep the small craft of the ORS *Chasseur* capable of spaceflight, often developing loving, paternal affection for their charges. The pilots then proceeded to take their precious small craft into danger, shooting recklessly and performing dangerous maneuvers and all manner of horrible things and would come back proud—*proud*—of how much damage they had taken without crashing, expecting the deck crew to just *fix* the craft so they could do it *again*! Hughes had actually had to physically restrain a deck chief once while Gutierrez made a strategic retreat.

"All right, Chief, all right," Ryu said. "We'll finish pre-flight up here, then we'll fix the gravity coil. Come on, Miranda." Ryu turned in her seat and started checking status lights on her control console. Sheepishly Gutierrez turned back to her own console as well. Hughes loomed there, as any good Chief Petty Officer knew how to do, and once satisfied that they were back to work he left them to it.

Gods know we don't need anything going wrong on this *flight*, he thought. *Now I just have to find gunny and make sure she has her marines ready. Maybe then I can shake this feeling of impending doom that's been nagging me all day.* Hughes stepped out of the landing craft to see Captain Jamie White, hero of the Orion Republic, approaching. He briefly considered ducking back inside the craft but decided to rip this particular metaphorical bandage off earlier rather than later.

"Ah, Chief Hughes! I was hoping to get to speak with you!" Captain White said amiably. The captain said everything amiably, which was a truly astounding talent, going through life as if everyone was a friend, even the ornithians who very much were *not* friends with *any* humans. A combination of effortless charisma and rugged good looks had made Captain White a media darling. "I'm looking forward to this peace talk with the ornithians! It's well past time we put to rest that old business."

First contact between the human Orion Republic and the aliens known as the ornithians had happened two years ago and ended rather disastrously. Hughes and Captain White had actually been present at the conference, although Hughes's memories were far more cynical than the captain's. A low-intensity war had broken out consisting of skirmishes and small raids between the two cultures but now the ornithians had requested parley.

"Yes, sir, although I am concerned that they asked for you personally. We know so little about the ornithians, it's impossible to guess their motives—"

"Yes, yes, all very mysterious. Nothing to worry about, though. The first step always begins with talking. Oh, there's a message for you from Fleet Command. Something about protocol?"

Hughes carefully kept any expression from appearing on his face. "Ah, yes, I should probably see to that before we head down to the surface. Captain." Hughes gave a salute and headed towards the goat locker.

It is a fact of most large organizations that the majority of work was accomplished not by the top-level brass but by people floating around in to the middle of the hierarchy. Those with enough authority to get others do to what needed to be done, but not subject to the outside scrutiny that being the head of any organization invariably brings. The crew of the ORS

Chasseur was no exception. Orders may come from the bridge, but decisions were made in the NCO wardroom. Part of a tradition handed down from the ocean-going navies of Earth, the goat locker was sacrosanct to the senior NCOs and not even Captain White could enter without permission.

Hughes scanned the wardroom as he entered and was relieved to see Gunnery Sergeant Kimathi snacking on some fried plantains. "Gunny! I was hoping to speak with you. How are preparations for today's drop?"

"I've got my best squad kitting up right now. I was about to head down and join them. You got one of your feelings again?" Hughes had an infamously honed sense of self-preservation for a senior Fleet non-com. Even a subconscious recognition of a detail that wasn't right could prove the difference between life or death.

"The whole situation has given me the heebie jeebies," he admitted. "We haven't had a single message from the ornithians in two years and now they want to talk. Feels out of character for them."

"I think you're overanalyzing again," Kimathi said as she stood up and placed her plate in the dishwasher. "I'm sure the ornithians are just as varied and complex as we humans are. I mean, could you imagine if humans all had the same character as the Captain?"

"Gods forfend us from such a fate."

"Oh, that's right." Kimathi snapped her fingers. "I just remembered. Message came in the SCIF for you from Command."

"Yeah, Captain gave me the same message. I'll see what they want and then meet you in the ready room. You have a spare set of body armor I can borrow?"

"Yeah, we have nice soft blankets too if it'll make you feel better." Kimathi winked at Hughes and headed out of the room. Hughes turned towards the gray steel cylinder that was the SCIF. Officially, the *Chasseur* and all other ships of her class had exactly one SCIF, located near the bridge up in officer country. Officers, after all, need to have access to classified information or what was the point of being one? But once again, the practical needs of reality trumped whatever regulations allegedly said.

Hughes sealed himself inside the SCIF. The exact composition of its walls was a tightly guarded secret but some combination of alloys ensured the space inside was an impenetrable void to eavesdroppers both organic and electronic; Fleet R&D also claimed it was impervious to psychic intrusion as well but how they tested *that* remained unknown. The one exception to this communication blackout was the quantum entanglement of an ansible. Even within a SCIF a matched pair of ansibles would communicate perfectly anywhere in the explored universe.

Hughes activated the ansible and contacted Fleet Command back on Earth. He patiently went through all the recognition codes which verified he truly was Chief Petty Officer Axel Hughes, serial number AH2479226, and finally got the welcome screen for Fleet Command. After a brief wait the screensaver was replaced with Commodore Nguyen, chief of Naval Intelligence. Hughes saluted. "Xir, I was told you had a matter of Protocol you needed to discuss with me?"

"Hughes, good to see you. Yes, it's Protocol, as if we ever talked about anything else. What do you know about these peace talks?"

"Not much that hasn't been shared in the media. We brought the diplomats onboard and have been heading for Kepler-62f.

They haven't interacted with the crew at all so what our actual objectives are I am sadly and entirely ignorant."

"Well now, that depends on who you ask, doesn't it?" From the outside the Orion Republic appeared to be a solid entity, humanity finally united as they pushed their way onto the galactic stage. In reality humanity remained just as divided as they had been since the Stone Age, they just hid it better now. The Republic's parliament had at least five major parties, and countless smaller ones, all trying to steer humanity in what they believed to be the correct direction. Then there was the inevitable conflict between the civilian members of parliament and the military professionals in Fleet, to say nothing of Fleet's own internal factions.

"What do we, by which I mean Naval Intelligence, want from this meeting, then, xir?"

"The war's been inconclusive so far, very low-intensity. Which suited our purposes very well, but the media's stopped paying attention. Protocol says we need to turn the heat up a bit. Fortunately we may have some unintentional help from the ornithians for that. Our cryptography department broke a fresh batch of ornithian communiques and it turns out a faction of their military wants to sabotage the peace talks."

"Convenient when the aliens do our work for us. And if they don't succeed?"

"Feel free to use your initiative. The level of skill which you used during the first contact with the ornithians was truly impressive, we at Naval Intelligence have every faith in your abilities. I'm sure you won't disappoint us."

Hughes smiled as he saluted. "Very well, xir."

* * *

"I hope everybody's strapped in back there!" Ryu called back from the flight deck. "We're hitting a lot of unexpected turbulence." The landing craft rocked again somewhat alarmingly and Hughes had to take another deep breath and another verse of *Rocket Rider's Prayer* came to his mind.

Now we're coming down from orbit, back to where the air is thick
With no engines and the glide path of a highly polished brick
And with nothing but those tiles between our hides and flaming Hell
Better pray to Hell's own Pluto that they glued those suckers well

Despite having survived eight combat drops, Hughes had never gotten the hang of orbital insertion. After careful consideration with a Fleet psychologist the conclusion was that his anxiety stemmed from the fact that he was in a situation he couldn't control. So he focused on things he could control. He triple-checked the restraints of his crash chair and, satisfied they were all in place, centered himself with breathing.Captain White, of course, was enjoying this experience immensely.

"Really invigorating, isn't it, Hughes?" he asked, speaking a little too loudly for the close confines of the passenger compartment. "Really makes you feel alive, not knowing what will happen next? By God, you have to do something like this every now and again, even when you're in command. Although I'm sure this is just another Tuesday to you fellows, eh?" White slapped Gunny Kimathi on the arm and the sergeant managed a smile which did not extend to her eyes. One member of her squad was deeply invested in a paper book while the rest had the bored look of people waiting to be somewhere else.

"Yes, sir," Kimathi answered. "Although, as I'm sure Chief Hughes has told you, your presence on this drop truly isn't necessary. My squad is perfectly capable of protecting the diplomats." Said diplomats were currently making use of the vomit bags provided to them before they entered the landing craft. Hughes suspected Ryu and Gutierrez were making this landing rough specifically to mess with the civilians. He was going to have to have words with them again.

"Nonsense! What sort of captain would I be if I refused to accompany my guests to their destination?"

One with more than a room-temperature IQ for starters, Hughes had tried, from the moment they had left Delta Base to their arrival in orbit here over Kepler-62f, to talk Captain White out of coming down with the diplomatic mission but all his efforts had failed. *Hopefully he'll get to see the aliens, deliver some sort of dramatic line he's been working on for the past week, and then he'll let the diplomats get on with the real work. It should make good copy for the news services.*

"We're coming up on the LZ," Ryu announced from the flight deck. "We should be on the ground in five minutes." Hughes offered up a silent prayer to all the gods and the diplomats let out a ragged chorus of "hooray".

It was pleasant in the particular part of Kepler-62f they landed on, temperature was somewhere around 20 degrees and it was a bright, sunny day with low humidity. Once they had recovered from the trip down, the diplomats looked rather happy to be dirtside again. Captain White was happy, but he would have been happy in the middle of a blizzard or a hurricane. Nothing penetrated White's shield of calm imperturbability and Hughes knew this from hard experience.

The ornithian lander came down from orbit, setting down across the meadow from the human party. Hughes made a note of how similar in design the ornithian craft was to their own. Despite differences in biology, the harsh rules of physics seemed to require similar engineering solutions. The craft's antigravity field didn't disturb so much as a blade of grass as it came down and landed with barely a sound. Hughes got the distinct impression the ornithians had seen the humans' landing and their pilot decided to show these deranged apes how it was really done.

Eventually the boarding ramp hissed open and the humans got their first sight of living ornithians. Hughes suspected Loki or Coyote or some other trickster god had a lot of fun setting this meeting up. The ornithians were most easily described as "utahraptors with the plumage of tropical macaws" and Hughes couldn't disagree. The ornithians advanced in a wedge formation and at the point of the wedge was a two-meter tall ornithian with bright scarlet, green, and blue plumage garbed in a robe of almost brilliant white. Behind the leader were ranks of ornithians whose feathers were a riot of reds, yellows, greens, blues, and even some purples. Silently, Hughes noted that while there seemed to be no hierarchy in color, the ornithians closest to the tip of the wedge had robes in off-whites or lighter shades of gray, while those towards the back had robes in dark grays heading towards almost black.

Outright black was reserved for the military class, who made the forward edges of the wedge. These ornithians were not dressed in robes but matte black armor which was designed for their saurian bodies. In their three-taloned hands they grasped what Hughes could only assume were weapons, though he couldn't begin to guess how they functioned. The party of ornithians stopped their advance upon reaching the exact halfway point of the meadow. After an awkward pause where the humans looked at each other, Captain White stepped up and the rest of the humans hurried to follow.

Hughes noted the camera drones managed to get into position for a good view of Captain White striding up boldly to the ornithians. He hadn't figured out which of the civilians among the diplomatic party was the press agent, but they were determined to get footage for their newsfeed. And White looked good walking, even Hughes had to admit to that. But that was the whole point, White looked good and got all the attention from the media, while the actual hard work got done by someone else.

When he was within a meter of the lead ornithian White stopped and spoke in his perfect Standard pronunciation. "Greetings, I am Captain White of the Republic starship *Chasseur*. We come here today in hopes of establishing a lasting peace between our two peoples." The words said, White gave his perfect smile and stood at parade rest while the ornithians translated.

After a pause for translation the scarlet ornithian at the head of the delegation began to speak. The ornithian language was a strange series of whistles, clicks, and squawks which bore a superficial resemblance to the sounds of birds from Earth. One of the diplomats whose name Hughes had never caught listened carefully and she began to translate. "Greetings, humans, we are pleased by your wisdom in seeking peace. For too long our nests have attacked each other to no benefit. We are pleased to see the humans are willing to accept our demand for negotiation."

The translator frowned in confusion as the ornithian leader continued. "Captain Jamie White, we hereby arrest you for the murder of Leader Jewel-of-Dawn and acts of terrorism." Two of the black-clad ornithians advanced, clearly intent on seizing

White.

"Now hold on just a minute!" White exclaimed, his un-flappable calm finally broken by this turn of events. "I don't remember killing any Jewel-of-Dawn person. What is the meaning of this?"

"Two years ago you sabotaged diplomatic talks between our peoples on the Planet of Twin Sunrises by murdering Jewel-of-Dawn. As a condition of peace talks with your government we demanded your extradition to our nest to stand trial." The soldier ornithians advanced again and laid hands on Captain White.

"Listen, I don't have any memory of killing this Jewel-of-Dawn fellow and I'm fairly certain I would if I did! Get off me!" White tried to fight off the ornithians but they were too quick and surprisingly strong for their wiry frames. In a matter of moments they had Captain White pinned and had started frog-marching him towards their ship. The diplomats were making protests and the conversation was going too quickly for Hughes to follow.

"Chief, what do we do?" Sergeant Kimathi asked. She had the nervous energy of a predator about to spring into action. She was already drifting into the fugue of battlespace, identifying targets, planning tactics.

Hughes's mind raced. *Was this the sabotage Nguyen warned me about? Or had Parliament made this deal and refused to tell Fleet?* Hughes looked over the diplomats, most of whom looked confused and were protesting vigorously. *Except for their leader. Minister... damn, what's his name? Well that's not important now, but* he *certainly doesn't look shocked by any of this. Still, we can't have Captain White dragged away in chains.* "Gunny Kimathi, rescue Captain White. Use of proportionate force is authorized.

Engage."

Within seconds of Hughes saying the words, Kimathi and her squad of marines reacted. Coilguns snapped from parade rest to firing positions and each marine began firing short, surgical bursts above the heads of the ornithians. The diplomats, both human and ornithian, screamed in surprise and dove for the ground, many of them covering their heads. The two ornithians carrying away Captain White let go long enough for their charge to start fighting them. Despite his flaws, Captain White was proficient in hand-to-hand combat and the ornithians were soon having the worse of the encounter.

There is a tremendous amount of wiggle room in the words "proportionate force," which made it a favorite of Naval Intelligence. A more intelligent and precise order would probably say something like "non-lethal force," making it clear the person giving the order did not intend to start killing. But proportionate force, well that leaves it up to the judgment of the marine on the spot. And if the other side starts trying to kill you then you kill them right back.

The ornithian soldiers reacted as most soldiers do and began firing their own weapons, which appeared to be some sort of energy weapon based on the purple lasers they emitted. One marine fell to the ornithians' fire, a charred hole in the center of her chest where the laser had punched through. The marines stopped firing over the ornithians' heads and the many hours of marksmanship training paid off as one after another the ornithians fell to their disciplined fire. *Their blood is red, like ours. Interesting.* It was a strange thing to notice at a time like this, with death all around him, such a trivial detail of biology.

"Hughes! Get down or shoot back already!" Kimathi managed to snap Hughes out of his disassociation and he assessed the battlefield. The ornithians were running back towards their ship, all semblance of order gone. The remaining soldiers fired their purple lasers at the humans as the diplomats scrambled up the boarding ramp. In the center of the crowd Hughes could see the scarlet and gold uniform of Captain White being dragged along by the ornithians into their ship.

On the human side, two marines had been downed, but Kimathi and the remaining eight were advancing on the ornithians. One group of marines would keep up a steady fire with their coilguns, forcing the ornithians to take cover or fire back; the second group would advance, take up position, and begin firing again. The human diplomats had already fled back into the landing craft, whether any of them were dead or wounded Hughes had no idea.

"Chief Hughes!" Ryu's voice came over the comm and Hughes had yet another problem to focus on. "The diplomats are demanding they take us back up to *Chasseur*. They say two of them are wounded and might die if they don't get emergency care. I can't get a hold of Captain White. What are your orders?"

"Have Gutierrez give them first aid. If they're not dead already, I doubt they're in any danger of dying soon. Get prepared for liftoff, but you don't leave without my orders, understood?" Hughes unholstered his own sidearm. Unlike the marines, Hughes had chosen an antique gunpowder weapon. There had been improvements over the centuries since its first production in 1911, but the essentials of the Colt .45 remained the same.

"But the diplomats..."

"I don't give a good goddamn what they want, I've got rank here. Tell them you need to run pre-flight or something. If that doesn't work tell them to suck eggs." Hughes cut the contact to the lander and shouted at the marines. "To the captain!" He took the shooter's stance and fired at the ornithians. He didn't know if his pistol had any effect on the armor-clad ornithians but the noise certainly added to the confusion and panic.

Kimathi shouted an order and the marines let out an "Oorah" before charging directly at the ornithians. The ornithian soldiers formed a firing line, five meters away from the fleeing diplomats. The marines crashed into them like a bowling ball into ninepins. The ornithians tried to fight back but were on the ground within seconds, dead or dying. Hughes followed behind, pausing to double-tap an ornithian that was trying to get back up. When Hughes looked up again, the marines had already broken into the mass of alien diplomats and were busy extracting Captain White from their clutches. Hughes tapped his comm. "Ryu, stand by for lift off, we'll be bringing the captain aboard momentarily."

It was at that moment that the ornithian ship exploded.

Hughes was thrown to the ground from the blast wave, stunned by this unexpected development. "Chief, are you still alive? Please respond! Chief? Gunny? Anybody?" Ryu's panicked voice was coming over his comm and Hughes struggled to reply.

"Third Squad, report!" came Sergeant Kimathi over the comm, apparently achieving the rank of Gunnery Sergeant made one immune to explosions. Hughes heard the marines reporting in and tried to keep count. *There seemed to be five? Maybe six? There had been eight before, right? Where is my comm at?* Hughes finally managed to stand up and see what the hell had just happened.

The ornithian ship was now a wreck of twisted scrap metal,

which would certainly never fly again, much less achieve orbit. He didn't know how many ornithians were dead, but the bright, gaudy colors of their feathers made a strange juxtaposition to their scattered body parts. If Hughes were a philosophical man he probably could have found some deep truth in that. A few ornithians were still alive, pulling themselves to their feet and looking just as disoriented as Hughes felt.

"Hughes, we have the captain, but he's unresponsive. Almost definitely a concussion, but I don't know what else could be wrong. We need to get him to medical on the *Chasseur*." A marine had slung the captain in a fireman's carry and was heading back towards the lander. Kimathi gestured towards the remaining ornithians as Hughes approached. "What do we do with the rest of them?"

Whether it was the gods or random chance, by some miracle the scarlet-feathered leader of the ornithians was still alive, though looking far less regal than when they first arrived on this misbegotten rock. "Take the leader hostage, we may find them useful later on. As for the rest..."

One of the ornithians, probably a translator, started to object in their language of chirps and whistles. Without a second thought Hughes fired two rounds into the alien's torso and they were dead before they even hit the ground. "Anybody tries to stop us, kill them. Otherwise, let the aliens pick up their own people." The ornithians, shocked by this display of casual cruelty, watched helplessly as the humans made their preparations to leave.

Hughes and Kimathi made their final check on the boarding ramp of the lander. "Four marines and one diplomat dead. Three diplomats wounded, although none seriously. And then the captain," Kimathi said. "Not the worst price I've paid for when things go sideways."

"Still four letters we need to write home and we don't know *how* sideways everything has gone," Hughes said, and then spat onto the dirt of Kepler-62f. "Let's get off this gods-damned planet. Ryu, start liftoff."

"Copy that, Chief," Ryu said. Hughes pulled the closing lever and the ramp began to raise shut. Kimathi and Hughes returned to their seats and strapped in for the ride back.

* * *

The lander rattled and a proximity alarm went off. "What was that?" one of the diplomats asked, panic in their voice. The lander rattled again but aside from some routine military swearing no answer came from the flight deck. Hughes rolled his eyes and undid the restraints on his chair, carefully climbed up to the flight deck and took in the situation. *If you want something done right, leave it to Chief Hughes to do it, with all my copious free time.*

Flight Officer Gutierrez was desperately goosing the engines to get that extra bit of lift out of the antigrav coils so they could make their ascent into orbit. Flight Officer Ryu was entirely focused on deploying ECM as alarms continued to demand attention. But Hughes knew how to read a radar scope and as he looked over Ryu's shoulder he did not like what he saw. Six contacts, which the lander's computer had tagged as hostile red, were rapidly gaining on the lander. The lander rattled again and Hughes had to grab a railing to stay steady. "Status report," he said, relying on training to take over.

"Six hostiles inbound, first warning I got was a target lock alert. I started ECM but the misses are getting closer," Ryu said, not looking up from her console. The lander was unarmed so turning around and fighting their enemies was out of the question. Plus, the hostiles were probably ornithian strike craft so a lander stood very poor chances of fighting them toe-to-toe anyway. Contacting the *Chasseur* would be no help either; as a cruiser, it carried no strike craft of its own and its gun batteries were not designed to pick off strike craft in the atmosphere one by one.

"ETA to rendezvous with *Chasseur*?"

"I don't know!" Gutierrez said as she forced the lander into another evasive maneuver. "Every time I manage to gain some altitude they fire more missiles and I have to duck again."

Hughes stumbled to where he could look over Gutierrez's shoulder and see her readouts. "Just redline the antigrav. It'll last long enough for us to get into orbit." There was a pause as Gutierrez very pointedly didn't say anything. "You didn't recalibrate the antigrav coil like I told you to, did you?"

"It was within tolerances! I thought this would be a nice, simple, diplomatic run! I didn't expect to be dodging strike craft!" The warning tone that an enemy had gotten target lock on them chimed and Gutierrez had to make the lander dive once again. Hughes nearly toppled over but was able to grab a handhold and remain upright.

"You want something done right," he muttered as he picked up the emergency toolkit stowed on the flight deck. Hughes headed back down into the main compartment while the lander continued to shift under him, but Hughes was in his element now. There was a crisis, there was a problem, and he could solve it. He managed to make it to where the troublesome antigrav coil was located and magnetically clamped the toolbox to the deck. It was one of the simpler, smarter developments of Fleet equipment; nobody wanted their wrenches and screwdrivers getting thrown all over the place in a combat situation.

Carefully Hughes removed the screws holding the panel in place and lifted it, revealing the antigrav coil. Despite being a Chief Petty Officer, Hughes couldn't explain exactly how the antigrav tech functioned. A very large amount of math went into it as well as physics, but the important thing was that Hughes knew how to calibrate the damn thing so he got to work. As he worked another verse of the song that had been pestering him all day came to mind.

As we're blasting off it's Mercury who'll help us in our need
Not only as the patron god of health and flight and speed
We hope that he will guard us as we're starting on this trip
As the god of thieves and liars like the ones who built this ship

Hughes concentrated on the hum of the coil as he adjusted it, listening as the pitch changed. Part of Fleet lore passed down from old hands to new was the exact frequency an antigrav coil would emit where you could get maximum lift out of it. The panic in the passenger compartment, the shifts of the lander below him, all of that disappeared as he focused on this one critical task. He heard the coil's hum change and he shouted to the flight deck, "REDLINE IT! NOW!" The lander groaned in protest and Hughes was pinned to the floor by at least three Gs of acceleration. Soon, the sounds from the outside ceased as the ship ascended into the vacuum of space and the extra weight from their mad dash into orbit let up as well.

Hughes climbed to his feet, putting the tools away but leaving the panel open. The antigrav would need replacing after a maneuver like that anyway. Hughes would even tell the deck crew not to give Gutierrez flak about it. Well, not *too* much. He made his way back to his seat and collapsed into it exhausted. The adrenaline was rapidly wearing off and he would have to check himself for shock once they docked with *Chasseur*. "ETA to *Chasseur*, five minutes," Ryu announced from the flight deck. "I let them know we have wounded inbound and hostiles after us." And Hughes found himself, however briefly, with nothing to do.

* * *

Hughes headed directly for the SCIF after docking with the *Chasseur*, not even bothering to remove his body armor. The sooner he made his report to Commodore Nguyen, the sooner NavInt could start spinning the situation to their advantage. Once he got to the NavInt screensaver, he actually had to wait half an hour before the commodore responded. It seemed the shit had already hit the fan as far back as Earth itself. "Hughes, glad to see you're alive," Nguyen said when xey finally appeared on the ansible screen. "I'm hoping you can tell me what the hell actually happened dirtside. Your XO's report left a lot to be desired."

"Well, you can hardly blame her. She wasn't there." Commander Pavlichenko had been extremely distracted evading the ornithians' strike craft as well as their mothership before making the FTL jump. Hughes imagined her report to headquarters was perfunctory at best considering how little time there had been to make one. "The ornithians arrested Captain White before they started negotiations, said he had something to do with the death of Jewel-of-Dawn. I don't know who Jewel-of-Dawn was, but I assume they were one of the leaders we assassinated on Brahe. We didn't leave any survivors of the Brahe peace talk, though. Could there be a leak in our operational security?"

Nguyen frowned in thought. "An unknown leak is the most likely possibility. The ornithians may have found out through other means as well. I'll need to start raising some hell and getting some answers. This is the first I heard that we were going to hand over Captain White to the ornithians as well."

"The chief diplomat didn't seem terribly surprised by the development, so I think Parliament agreed to sacrifice Captain White for the greater good. Oh, that sabotage you warned me about happened. The ornithians' landing craft exploded."

Nguyen swore in xeir native language and rubbed xeir eyes. "What a mess. Too many factions fighting each other, why can't I have nice, tidy monoliths. So you rescued Captain White from the vile clutches of the aliens?"

"We did, at the cost of four marines and some unknown number of aliens. Oh, I took their leader hostage as well, for all the good it did us. I have them isolated in the brig for now and I ordered the marines to shoot any diplomats that try to talk to them."

"Excellent! Maybe we can finally get some answers. I'll have a black site team waiting for them when you dock." Even if the diplomats told their superiors in the civilian side of the Orion Republic that a prominent ornithian had been taken captive, it was very unlikely Parliament would be able to find this ornithian ever again. The last thing anybody in NavInt wanted Parliament to get was direct, unfettered access to an ornithian with authority.

"Very good, xir. In the meantime, do you have any other

tasks you need me to complete?"

"No. I still have a great many questions but I know who to ask, which is a considerable improvement. And Protocol is satisfied because the war continues. Your work, as always, Hughes is commendable. Nguyen out."

* * *

"What's his prognosis?" Hughes asked. After completing his call with Commodore Nguyen, Hughes headed down to medical to check on Captain White. Dr. Ortega was still working on him, carefully scanning the captain's head.

"I've seen worse but that's not encouraging with head wounds," they said, not looking up from the scanner's display screen. "He has a serious concussion from the blast and there's significant swelling in his cranium. I'm trying to figure out of it's bad enough that I need to go in and operate." The scanner beeped and Dr. Ortega stopped, looking at the readout with confusion. "That makes no sense, why is there no record of this? It should be in his chart if nothing else." Ortega turned to a computer console and brought up Captain White's chart, scanning through all the major operations. "You don't just put a chip in somebody's head and don't leave a *record*. That's just bad medical practice. What if he'd needed an MRI?"

Ortega's verbal train of thought was stopped by Hughes placing a hand over their own. "Doctor, let me give you some advice, one Fleet veteran to another. Don't go digging into this and don't leave a record that you found it. Forget it's even there."

"But he's had a brain injury! And now I'm finding out my patient has a brain chip that's appeared from God alone knows where."

"Doctor, this is so classified that even knowing how classified it is requires a higher security clearance than you have. Forget that it was ever a thing." Hughes voice was flat, but it held a trace of menace. It was common knowledge on the *Chasseur* that Hughes was a spook; every ship in the Fleet had at least one. Ironically people knowing you were a spook often left you free to do your work in peace. But nobody on board had any clue exactly how high in NavInt Hughes was.

Dr. Ortega put their thoughts in order before responding. "All right, I'll try to work around it for now. But that concussion may have done damage to the chip. I may still have to go in and take it out if the Captain doesn't improve."

"Notify me before you do. And, doctor, this stays between us. Not even the XO can find out. Understood?" As a lieutenant, Dr. Ortega outranked Hughes and there was nothing within the letter of regulations which could keep them from going directly to Commander Pavlichenko and revealing everything. But Ortega merely nodded in assent. Petty Officers formed their own hierarchy, regardless of what naval regulations said. "Good, keep me informed of the captain's status."

* * *

They were three days back towards Republic space when all hell broke loose. Hughes was, as he often was when he had a spare moment, in the goat locker catching up on the various paperwork that accrues within any military. The ship's intercom chimed and the computer's voice announced "Medical to Chief Hughes."

"Put me through, Majel," Hughes replied.

"Hughes, the captain's gone!"

"Gone? What do you mean gone? He died?"

"No! He was still alive last I checked, but he's disappeared from Medical!" Dr. Ortega's voice was panicked. "He hasn't responded to any external stimulus for days and now he's gone."

"I'm on my way." Hughes got up, paperwork forgotten, and started jogging towards Medical. Hughes unlocked his communicator as he ran, first contacting the ship's computer. "Majel, lock Captain White's access to all vital systems. Authorization: Hughes, 2479226."

The computer made a small chirp, affirming it had received and understood its orders. "Captain White is currently using the console in his quarters. Should I deny him all access?"

"What's he doing?"

"Researching his service record and attempting to access classified files."

Hughes paused in his run. With the captain locked out of vital systems he couldn't deactivate the magnetic fields around the fusion reactor and blow the *Chasseur* to Hades. On the other hand, with computer access and a little creativity, there was a lot of havoc someone could cause with even non-vital systems. "As long as he's just looking at records it's fine. Cut his access to comms and all other systems and lock him inside his quarters. Key the lock to my DNA signature, I don't want anyone else getting in or out."

"Understood. There are also two wounded crew members outside Captain White's quarters and Yeoman Lee is inside. I have reason to believe he's armed."

"Oh, I don't like that. I don't like that at *all*. Hughes to Medical."

"Ortega here."

"Good news, Majel found the captain. Bad news, he's locked in his quarters with a hostage and he's wounded two crew. I need a response team up to his quarters stat."

"Understood, Ortega out." It seemed Ortega's initial panic had subsided and Hughes had no doubt their cool professionalism would resurface. That was the benefit of Fleet training: you didn't have to think during a crisis, you just did what was expected of you.

"Hughes to Commander Pavlichenko."

"Pavlichenko here. Hughes, this had better be important, I finally fell asleep." With the captain unavailable, the watch schedules for officer country had undergone an adjustment. Pavlichenko in particular had not been pleased by this change.

"The captain's awake, he's armed, and he has a hostage. He's locked in his quarters for now, we're on our way to handle the situation. Whatever you do, *do not* listen to any orders he might give."

"I'm sorry, Captain White took a hostage?" All sleepiness was gone from Pavlichenko's voice. "He raided an arms locker and took a hostage. What sort of brain damage did he get on Kepler-62f?"

"That is an excellent question that Dr. Ortega will be trying to answer. I'll give status updates as I get them. Hughes out." Hughes changed his route, the trip to medical no longer being necessary. Instead, he headed directly for the marines' armory. Gunny Kimathi would be off-duty right now, but somebody would be there to help him. Inside the armory he found a corporal, someone whose name he could never remember, doing equipment inspections. "How many marines are on duty right now?" Hughes asked without preamble.

She looked up, surprised, and managed to stammer a response "We should have fifteen, sir, Chief Hughes, sir. Second and Fifth Squads are on duty at the moment, but some marines from Fifth got moved to Third and…"

"Thank you, corporal. I need…yes, just a fireteam will be sufficient. I will also need body armor and a sidearm."

"Is everything all right, Chief?"

"Captain's gone crazy and taken hostages, I'm defusing the situation." That was all the explanation Hughes offered and he found the body armor he had worn just the other day on Kepler-62f. By the time Hughes finished suiting up five grim-faced marines had joined him. Hughes addressed them as they made their own preparations. "All right, I don't expect any of you to help me take down the captain. I'm going to get Yeoman Lee out and try to talk the captain down. I want you to secure the perimeter but if you see the captain make a break for it you're to shoot first and ask questions later, understood?"

The marines looked at each other nervously before the Corporal, Ellison was her name, spoke up. "Chief, can you tell us *why* we're shooting the captain? That's usually a court-martial offense with the penalty of getting drummed out of the corps and spending the rest of your life dirtside in a prison on a high-g world."

Hughes decided, in time honored fashion, to use a partial truth to enable a greater lie. "Doctor Ortega located a chip in Captain White's brain. We're not sure where it came from or who put it there, but we think the ornithians may have activated some sort of sleeper protocol. Until we can get him back to more sophisticated medical facilities we just don't know the danger."

That was enough to assuage any lingering doubts the marines had and they followed Hughes up to Officer Country. On the way there, they met Ortega wheeling a loaded gurney towards the nearest lift. Behind them was a medic with a second gurney. "No major organs or arteries hit, thank God," Ortega said, crossing themself. "The bullets were already spent, if I had to guess they got hit by ricochets. Lucky for them."

"Would have been luckier if they hadn't been hit at all," Hughes said as the two casualties were taken away. At least that would be two less letters home he'd have to write. With a series of hand signals he directed the marines to fan out through the corridors. Any officers who were in this part of the ship were wisely remaining inside their quarters with the doors locked, eager to avoid catching a bullet themselves. It was eerily quiet on a ship where, even in the depths of "night," people were awake.

Hughes walked up to the captain's quarters without making a sound. Two dark red blood stains on the deck indicated where the unfortunate crewmembers had fallen. "Majel," Hughes subvocalized so that only the ship's computer could hear him. "Turn off all recording devices in the captain's quarters."

"I am sorry," Majel replied. "I am unable to comply with that request. Per Fleet Regulation 18 dash—"

"Emergency Override, Eschatology Protocol, Sudo make me a sandwich."

"Emergency Override recognized, all recording devices have been turned off."

Hughes checked his weapon, ensuring he had a round in the chamber and paused. When he had first joined Fleet, religion had still been a part of daily life for him, but the demands of Fleet life had made it difficult to keep up the complex series of rituals he had grown up with. Fleet did not recognize the complex calendar of holy days his family had kept, adjusted from Earth standard to the small moon they'd settled on. Limited living space on ships meant keeping a personal altar was impossible and frequent reassignments meant personal possessions were just one more thing to pack. To some extent, his religion had been eroded by the pressures of Fleet life, but from time to time it bubbled to the surface. *If there are any gods out there listening,* he thought, *I could use a little bit of divine intervention right about now.*

"Majel, unlock the door to the captain's quarters and then lock it again once I'm inside."

"Understood."

Hughes waited for the status light next to the captain's door turn green, then opened the hatch and pulled it closed behind him. The locks clunked into place and Hughes lifted his pistol to the ready position. Space was always a premium so although Captain White had the luxury of multiple rooms, one of them functioned as a combination of his living room/dining room/office; it was currently in shambles. Hard copy printouts from the computer terminal were scattered across the floor of the chamber, a great number of them wadded up into balls before being thrown in one corner. Most of the furniture had been pushed to one side and in a clear spot devoid of papers was a complex diagram drawn in markers of various colors. Tied to one of the chairs with what appeared to be ripped bed linens was Yeoman Lee. Lee also had a makeshift gag shoved into his mouth so all he could do upon seeing Hughes was make a muffled, inarticulate shout. Hughes tried to gesture for Lee to shut up but it was too late.

"Hughes! I had been wondering when you'd be joining us. Come in, come in. Let's have ourselves a long overdue chat." Captain White stepped into Hughes's view. This man was nothing like the amiable buffoon who had gone down to the surface of Kepler-62f. His eyes had a sharp, calculating intelligence that had *never* been present in the years Hughes had known him. White had changed into a fatigue uniform, his blood-splattered white medical smock hanging incongruously on a coat hook behind him. White held a pistol in his left hand, almost absentmindedly, as if he'd forgotten he even had it. "Oh, you can lower your firearm, Hughes. We won't be shooting each other. Not yet. I suspect you have some questions for me as well."

Keep him talking, Hughes thought. *That's how you get out of this situation. You listen to the madman's little pet theory while you look for opportunities. The longer he talks, the more time you get.* Hughes lowered his gun about ten centimeters but remained ready to snap back into position."Well, I suppose my first question, sir, should be how are you feeling?"

White laughed bitterly. "Funny you should ask that, Hughes. Funny you should ask that. You know, I am feeling like a fog has lifted from my mind for the first time in almost twenty years. I was towards the top in my class from the academy, did you know that? Right there in my dossier, but you've read it plenty of times."

"That's…good? Sir?" Hughes had an inkling of where this was going but he didn't want to give away more information than he had to.

"Flagged for the fast-track to promotion and command, I'd be one of the youngest Fleet captains in history. Nothing but glory ahead of me. But then the accident happened." White gave a wry chuckle. "It wasn't all that surprising, not even to my own parents bless their souls. I had been out drinking with my friends celebrating the end of exams and the start of our careers. I made the mistake of driving home that night, and I had gotten so blackout drunk that I didn't remember what happened until I woke up in a hospital with a head injury."

"But you know, reading the accident report things don't quite add up." The captain bent over and picked up a sheet of paper. "It says here they found my groundcar smashed into a jersey barrier. Based on the damage they estimated I had been going 120 kilometers an hour when I hit it. But you know the weird thing? The really weird thing, was that I was found inside the vehicle without my seat belt fastened. Going at that speed I should have flown through the windshield and landed…How far did you say it was, Lee?"

There was a muffled, terrified response from Lee but it didn't seem to matter. "That's right, several meters at least. But now, I was inside my vehicle with just a head injury."

"Well, you know, small miracles happen all the time," Hughes said.

"The airbags didn't deploy either," the captain said, derailing Hughes's answer. "But the police didn't ask any questions, just took me to the nearest Fleet hospital. It took some serious pulling of strings to keep me from getting kicked out of Fleet entirely."

"Well you still managed to have a Fleet career," Hughes tried again. "Your superiors were perfectly justified in their faith of you, your record alone—"

"Yes, let's examine that record." White dropped the police report and hunted through his papers until he pulled up a sheet with numerous hand-written notations. "The workers' revolt on Wolf 1069b. Lieutenant Junior Grade White, bravely leading a team of marines, suppressed the revolt and brought the colony back under Republic control. That's the summary that the public's told anyway, and it's what I remembered. But you know, now I can seem to remember I ended the workers' revolt by massacring their leadership with the help of Chief Petty Officer Vandenburg. And wouldn't you know, there's a classified report from Chief Vandenburg about the incident."

Hughes knew the situation was approaching the point he couldn't salvage it, but he had to give it at least one more try. "Well, you know, memory is such a malleable thing. Perhaps reading the report made you *think* you remembered—"

"That would make sense, wouldn't it? But no, all of a sudden I had a flash of memory and I said to myself 'It couldn't have happened that way, could it?' Then I found Vandenburg's report. But that's not the only incident I have two sets of memories for. There's our recent misadventures with the ornithians, for example. We were together for that one, Hughes, two years ago. First contact with a new, alien species. Such a wonderful opportunity for humanity and it was such a shame that I ruined it by murdering Jewel-of-Dawn."

"I take it you found my report?" Hughes asked, deflated. It seemed NavInt was going to have to put a new level of security between their files and the rest of Fleet.

"Yes, with some rather glowing remarks from Commodore Nguyen, xey're rather proud of you as an operative." The captain picked up another piece of paper and began to read. "We have successfully assassinated the ornithian ambassador. The sleeper agent programming worked perfectly and as far as the ornithians are concerned, Captain White acted alone. In the ensuing chaos I was able to eliminate a number of other high-profile targets of opportunity which you can see in the attached list. Protocol can analyze the data but I don't see how the ornithians can ignore the provocation to war."

Captain White looked up from the paper. "There's that word, Protocol. With a capital P. It seemed such a strange thing for you to put into your report. But I noticed it once and then I started noticing it everywhere." He started pointing out parts of his complex diagram on the floor. "Wolf 1069b, worker's revolt considered by Protocol. Resources determined to be of absolute strategic necessity and revolt determined to have adverse effect on Protocol. Conquest of the Sirius Cluster, approved by Protocol as appropriate direction of energy and resources."

"It looks like every major decision the Republic has made in the past hundred years has been affected one way or another by Protocol. So that's what I want to know, Hughes. Who are these mysterious people pulling the strings? I think you know." In a surprisingly fluid motion White pointed his pistol directly at Hughes, his aim rock steady. "So start talking before I splatter your brains all over my cabin."

Hughes sighed. There really was no way out of it now. "Protocol refers to the Eschatology Protocol. It's a mathematical model that NavInt has been using to avoid humanity's self-destruction."

"By getting us involved in endless wars? How does that help us?"

"Captain, how much Earth history do you know? I know you took the core curriculum at the Academy but those chips play hell with your brain."

"I mean—I can remember broad strokes."

Hughes casually walked over to one of the captain's chairs and sat down, facing White. In his confusion White's pistol was no longer targeted at Hughes but pointing aimlessly at the floor again. "Going into the late 1900s there were two main superpowers on Earth, the United States of America and the Union of Soviet Socialist Republics. For forty years the conflicting ideologies between the two had driven them to new developments in science, technology, culture. The first Space Race! Before the billionaires came and ruined it. But then, in 1991, the Soviet Union disintegrated. The US stood triumphant, ushering in a new hegemony for the world. Humanity would enter a new century, a new millennium, and a new era of peace and prosperity without the threat of nuclear annihilation."

"I take it from your tone that didn't happen."

Hughes gave a derisive snort. "Of course not. Without an outside challenge the United States grew soft and complacent. Within thirty years the United States was on the brink of fracture because its people had turned on each other. And this is to say nothing about the late-stage capitalism they were going through."

"What does this have to do with Protocol?"

"I'm providing context to help you understand. So jump forward two hundred years: Humanity has put aside their differences on Earth and thanks to FTL drive we've spread out among the stars, colonizing distant worlds. Thanks to subspace communication and the ansible, we're united into one Republic. Except there's a problem. Fractures are starting to appear in the Republic. Nothing serious, but hairline cracks that could grow larger with time and stress. So Naval Intelligence creates a special group to create an Eschatology Protocol for use if the cracks start to get bigger."

"Eschatology? I'm not familiar with the word." White asked.

"Comes from ancient Greek, it's the study of the end of the world. Armageddon, Ragnarok, the End Times. They recognized that if the Republic grew complacent there was a possibility that it would collapse under internal divisions. To stave off this cataclysm, they needed to keep humanity united, and the easiest means was via an external threat. So they orchestrated a war with the myrmidons. It's in the bottom left corner of your diagram, by the way."

Captain White turned to the spot Hughes had indicated and picked up another printout. "I was going to ask about that. Why we declared war on space-faring ants that lived on planets with denser atmospheres than was comfortable for humans. If we were fighting over the same resources that would have made more sense…"

"The myrmidons were a prime first target for us. Physically weaker than humans, largely peaceful, concerned mostly with gathering food, caring for their young, doing math. They rather liked math. But humanity was already primed to hate them. Even before we had left Earth, humanity had dozens of stories of us fighting bug-like aliens. It was so very easy to tip popular opinion from a wary distrust into outright hate."

"So we murdered an entire species just to keep us from murdering ourselves?"

Hughes tsked disapprovingly as he leaned back in the chair and propped his feet up on the captain's table. "We didn't murder *all* of them. We're not complete monsters. There's a world where the myrmidons are kept under our watchful eye lest they rise up against us. Or we need them to rise up against us, but that would have been trickier to manage. The ornithians were a godsend in that regard, they've got far more fight in them than the myrmidons ever had. We can drag this conflict out as long as we need to. And you, my dear Captain White, have been so very helpful in making that happen."

"So the chip in my brain, that was what, to control me?" There were hints of rage in White's face now. Hughes could tell he was close to the tipping point; as always, White just needed a little push over the edge.

"In extreme circumstances. Mostly it made you more biddable, more likely to follow our suggestions and take the path we recommended. Less likely to ask inconvenient questions. A well-trained dog."

White screamed incoherently and fired his pistol into Hughes, aiming for the center of mass in a reflex shaped by Fleet training. Hughes tumbled backwards out of the chair and onto the floor, momentarily stunned but still alive. The body armor had done its job, and now it was time for Hughes to do his. Without a further comment he lifted his pistol and placed two well-aimed shots into White's stomach. White fell, clutching his stomach in agony as blood seeped from his wounds and stained the now scattered papers.

Slowly, with a bit of grunting on his part, Hughes got to his feet and stumbled over to where White was now curled up on the floor in excruciating pain. "And as every handler knows," he said, partly for White's benefit but mostly for his own, "sometimes you have to put a dog down." And then he pistol-whipped White, rendering the former captain unconscious. Hughes holstered his pistol and picked up White's own weapon. Hughes turned to the shocked and stunned Yeoman Lee.

"I am truly sorry about this. If I had been able to avoid talking about Protocol you would have survived this." Lee's eyes widened with shock and he tried to shout something before Hughes fired two shots into his head. Lee's body toppled over, taking the chair with it, and landed with a meaty thud on the deck. "Hughes to Medical."

"Ortega here."

"I've got one dead, one wounded. Captain White shot Yeoman Lee when I came in, I managed to give White a gutshot. I would recommend keeping him sedated until we make it back to Earth."

* * *

"Hughes! Glad to see you in one piece after that little incident on *Chasseur*!" Hughes saluted as Commodore Nguyen approached from across the landing bay. When the *Chasseur* had finally arrived in Earth orbit a secure NavInt shuttle had docked with the ship and ferried Hughes, the ornithian prisoner, and a heavily-sedated former Captain White to the far side of Luna.

"Thank you, xir. I know I can definitely use the two weeks of shore leave after I get finished with the debriefing."

"Should be mostly a formality. Your reports are detailed and yet concise as always. I already have people working on the holes in our OpSec and CompSec you pointed out. It will take us some time to scrub all of Fleet's servers, though. You're certain there are no other leaks?"

"As certain as I can be about anything. What'll happen to White?"

"We'll analyze the chip, try to figure out what went wrong, maybe fix it. If we can keep a lid on the incident we might be able to slip him back into service but it's too early to tell yet. You we're going to have to transfer regardless. Commander Pavlichenko started asking a lot of pointed questions about your exact role on the ship. I wonder why we never chipped her."

"Xir, we can't chip every officer in Fleet, we need to keep *some* competent officers around."

Nguyen sighed. "I suppose you're right, Hughes. Evil never sleeps and as a result NavInt works overtime." And so the wheels of bureaucracy turned.

Stolen and Broken Hearts

Anise looked at their clipboard for their last appointment of the day. Curses and magical afflictions had not been their specialization when they had first become a Learned, but in the city of Aelelea, it paid to diversify. The demand for illusions may come and go, but someone *always* needed a curse removed.

Anise poked their head into the waiting room and called, "Jack Green and Heliotrope?" An air pirate, identifiable by his cutlass and oxygen mask, stood up. He was dressed in a celadon green linen shirt and rifle green canvas trouser, tucked into knee-high boots and held up by an emerald green silk sash embroidered with golden thread tied tightly around his waist. He held a small wooden box with small holes drilled in the lid.

"Mr. Green, I assume." Anise said. "Are we still waiting for Heliotrope?"

"No, no, she's in the box," Jack explained and he opened the lid to reveal an angry, bright red poisonous frog.

Anise crossed their arms, peeved. "Mr. Green, you do understand that I am one of the Learned? If you need an exotic veterinarian I can recommend one just down the street."

"No, the problem is she's not always like this!" Jack explained. "She's been cursed."

"Oh, that I can help you with. Please step into my office."

Anise put on a pair of goggles, one lens tinted green, the other blue, and waited for Jack to place the box containing Heliotrope on the examination table. Without prompting Jack sat down in one of the chairs as Anise leaned over the table to get a good look. Anise's butterfly wings flapped in irritation as they examined the lines of magic surrounding the frog's body. "Good gods, this is one doozy of a curse. Just who did you piss off?"

"The Autumn Queen," Jack answered.

Anise lifted their goggles up so they could look directly at Jack. "I'm sorry, I'm having trouble hearing right now. Because I thought I just heard you say that you decided to fight the Autumn Queen."

"Heliotrope held a principality in the Autumn Court before she was—well—that," Jack said, pointing towards the box. The frog made a very grumpy-sounding ribbit.

Anise leaned against their examination table. "Listen here, buccaneer, I'm a Learned and even *I* wouldn't go up against the Autumn Queen without help from, oh, let's say at least two other Learned." Although the two Learned Anise had in mind could probably take one of the Seasonal Courts without her help.

Fae naturally gathered together in courts because it fed their passion for hierarchy and drama. Some, like the Court of Roses, were the equivalent of an amateur theatrical troupe; long on passion but short of everything else. The Seasonal Courts were the very end of the scale, recognized as sovereign nations and one you the monarch at your own peril. "Perhaps you could start at the beginning and explain to me how Heliotrope hasn't been rendered into her constituent atoms."

"All right, you have to understand that I wasn't actually there to see it happen," Jack said. "I came back from a raid with my crew. Heliotrope usually provides us a safe harbor between jobs, and this time we get intercepted by some knights of the Autumn Court riding griffins, demanding that we heave to. And I ain't about to sour relations for no good reason. Anyway, some bloke calling himself Duke Fife comes aboard and hands me this box saying Her Notul Majesty has exiled Heliotrope and as such the crew of the *Howling Banshee* are no longer welcome in her realm. And, well, I'm married to Heliotrope so I couldn't exactly abandon her as she is." It took considerable self-restraint from Anise to keep from rolling their eyes. Human-fae marriages always seemed to have an unnecessary amount of drama. "So we set course for Aelelea and you were the first curse-breaker I can find."

"Well, Mr. Green, I have good news and bad news regarding your spouse. The good news is that her curse is rather simple, the fae courts are always fans of tradition. Heliotrope can be returned to her regular form with a simple kiss. However—"

"She's a poison frog so if I kiss her I'll die," Jack said, completing Anise's sentence. Or so he thought.

"What? No, that's not it at all. Don't jump to conclusions," Anise said, annoyed by Jack's interruption. "The catch is that the curse can only be broken by the kiss of a true enemy. Someone who hates her with every fiber of their being. Or close enough so as to make no difference. Does she happen to have any enemies that fit the bill, Mr. Green?"

Jack bit his lip, hesitating to answer the question. "There might be one person who fits the bill. Is the Artificer still in town?"

* * *

"I still don't think we should go with you," Jack said, staying as far away from Anise as possible while still being able to be heard. "Seriously, I'll pay you to go for us while we wait at the docks."

"We'll waste who knows how much time running back and forth to get an answer," Anise said blithely over their shoulder as they hovered above the crowd. Their wings had originally been an affectation, an illusion designed to draw the eye, but with the help of other Learned Anise had managed to grow their own pair of wings and every moment of pain growing the damn things was, in their opinion, absolutely worth the ability to fly. Plus it made navigating Iron Street, the heart of Aelelea's workshop district and one of its most congested streets, all the easier. "Besides, the Artificer's really rather kind once you get past their curmudgeonly facade."

"Oh, I know," Jack said, trying to keep hold of the box containing Heliotrope as he dodged an automaton-pulled wagon. "Heliotrope was an intimate friend of the Artificer once. It's the reason why they're a candidate for breaking the curse that makes me worried." He followed Anise into a side alley and stopped, looking for some sort of cover. Unfortunately whoever used this alley believed in keeping it clear for regular traffic and none of the usual convenient detritus of barrels, crates, or random garbage were present. "Listen, if we could just wait here."

"It'll be fine!" Anise repeated, landing gently on the paving bricks and walking towards a steel door painted lapis blue. On the door was a series of letters carefully written in turquoise in a language lost a long time ago from a land far away from Aelelea. Some said it was the true name of the Cunning Artificer but Anise found that doubtful. The Artificer had gone a long way to hide their name so others couldn't use it, they certainly wouldn't leave it lying around where just anyone could see it.

Anise was about to knock on the door when a gunshot made them look up in surprise. Random explosions weren't rare in this part of Aelelea but this had the distinct sound of a ricocheting bullet. "That was a warning shot, Jack. Next bullet goes right between your thrice-damned eyes." The Artificer had a rifle propped on the windowsill above their front door. Somehow the click of the rifle's action being worked echoed above the noise of traffic outside the alley.

"Arty, you stop that," Anise said, using the nickname only the Learned on the friendliest of terms with the Artificer were allowed to use. "Jack and Heliotrope need your help. It won't take but a minute of your time."

"If I'd known Heliotrope was here, I wouldn't have wasted the warning shot. Where is she?"

"She's been turned into a frog, Arty. Listen, we can stand here in the alley and shout your business where everyone can hear or you can at least have the decency to invite us inside. Which would you prefer?"

There was a pause as the Artificer pretended to weigh their choices. Anise knew darn well that even if this enmity between the couple and Artificer was as vicious as Jack claimed, the Artificer would prefer to handle it privately. "Give me a minute," the Artificer grumbled and the window slammed shut with an angry thud. Anise waited patiently as the bolt behind the steel door turned and it finally opened, although with no Artificer in sight. They waved to Jack, who reluctantly followed inside, and entered the front office of the Artificer's workshop. This was as far as most people got into the Artificer's home and office. Of the countless denizens of Aelelea, maybe one in a hundred even knew where the Artificer lived. It was relentlessly professional. A great wooden desk faced the door with all the papers and drafting tools neatly arranged in their appropriate spots; Anise suspected Arty didn't have to dust their desk because dust was afraid to land on it. The walls were decorated with tastefully arranged framed prints of trains and various maps and a couple of comfortable if spartan chairs were scattered around for customers to sit during consultations. Anise had seen this room plenty of times and didn't even jump when the steel door slammed shut behind them.

"Arty, now is not the time to be playing silly games." Anise chided as they turned around. The Artificer, who had been hiding behind the door to make some sort of point, was about to argue before Anise interrupted. "You always hide behind the door when you're upset—why, I have no idea. I'm sure Teal could tell me if I really cared. Now Jack has been gracious enough to come all this way to ask for your help and I think you could at least do him the courtesy of hearing him out."

"Fine," the Artificer said, crossing the room and falling into their swivel chair behind the desk. "What disaster did you get yourself into this time?"

Jack opened the box and carefully placed Heliotrope on the desk blotter. Somehow despite being a frog, Heliotrope managed to look angrier than she had before. Jack briefly repeated the events as he'd told it to Anise and to their credit, the Artificer didn't interrupt once.

"Seems appropriate that Heliotrope got turned into a poison frog," Arty said once Jack's story was finished. "She certainly was toxic enough in her regular form. Sorry to hear about it, but you can go pound sand for all I care."

"Arty!" Anise exclaimed.

"What?"

Anise stood up and grabbed Arty's hand, pulling them to their feet. "Jack, will you wait here for a moment with Heliotrope?" Anise herded Arty into their reference library over Arty's continued protests, then shut the door to the library behind them. "I don't understand why this is such a problem for you!" Anise said as they turned on Arty, keeping their voice hushed to keep from carrying. "You do plenty of things out of the goodness of your heart every day, don't try to deny it."

"That may be so, but Heliotrope took that very same heart and put it into a blender. I wouldn't even piss on her if she was on fire. *And* she probably set herself on fire so she could play the victim."

"Arty! You're not usually this crass."

"Well, what do you want from me? You brought enemies into my home."

"I would appreciate it if you started with at least some civility." Anise flicked the Artificer's arm and they rolled their eyes in frustration. "All right, goodness of your heart completely off the table, is there *anything,* any mercenary desire in your heart of hearts, which Jack and Heliotrope could do to get you to help break the curse? And before you answer, Heliotrope taking a flying leap at the moon isn't an option."

"I wasn't going to say that!"

"No, you were thinking something I couldn't repeat in front of polite company."

The Artificer leaned against a bookcase crammed full of reference volumes, all of which they'd read and some of which they'd written themselves, and let out a frustrated sigh. "There is possibly *one* thing within Jack's power to accomplish which would allow me to unbend enough to grant their fairly limited request. I want a piece of the Heart of Hy-Brasil." The Artificer turned around and scanned the shelves before pulling down an atlas of various worlds adjacent to Aelelea. They scanned through the book until stopping at a specific page, propping the book open and showing it to Anise.

On the page was a line drawing of an island shrouded in mists. The center of the island was taken up by a great mountain covered with tropical trees, but the most unusual thing were airships cruising both above and below the island, an indicator that Hy-Brasil floated in the sky, rather than in the ocean as most islands did. "Inside the mountain there's a great stone which keeps the entire island floating," Arty explained. "The locals call it the Heart, pirates from all across the universe have set up on Hy-Brasil. They've turned it into a massive pirate base."

The Artificer set the atlas down and looked for another book, pulling a thin folio of blueprints from a shelf and opening them. They showed a diagram of an airship to Anise, this one was built more like a traditional sailing ship and did not have a gas bag or other obvious means of lifting itself. Arty pointed to a room towards the center of the ship labeled on the diagram as "Ship's Heart."

"The pirates have found a way to take pieces of the Heart and use them to power their airships. They've kept it a closely guarded secret, I only heard about these new sorts of ships five years ago and I still can only guess at how they work. If I have a piece of the Heart I can study it and figure out how they're getting those ships to fly."

"Oh, is that all?" Anise asked.

"Heliotrope has plenty of other enemies she can ask to break the curse. Well, Jack can ask them to do it. I don't know the path to Hy-Brasil but I can guarantee Jack does. He wants my help, he brings me a piece of the Heart."

* * *

"You really don't need to come with us," Jack said for probably the tenth time as they walked through Aelelea's bustling aerodrome. Fast little tugs helped guide great dirigibles into cavernous docking bays protected against the wind and elements. Flat expanses of tarmac allowed heavier-than-air vessels to land and take off in a carefully controlled chaos. Everywhere people and freight were being transferred from Aelelea's own rail network to travel to worlds where the skies were the highways of commerce.

"I'm curious about this Hy-Brasil. I'd like to see it with my own eyes," Anise said.

"Really, you've helped us enough so far, we really couldn't expect you to come with us."

"Captain Green," Anise used the courtesy of Jack's title as they entered his domain, "I am sensing that there is something else about Hy-Brasil which you're not telling me. Is it perhaps the fact that Hy-Brasil is extremely defensive against the encroachments of outsiders?"

At Jack's flummoxed expression Anise continued. "It's really not that hard to figure out. As a rule pirates are a superstitious and cowardly lot, so if they were to establish an entire pirate base on a semi-mythical flying island they would jealously guard that particular secret. For all the good it's done them. If Arty has a book about it, you can be sure there are hundreds of other people who know."

"I really don't know if I appreciate how you're characterizing my profession." Jack struggled to keep up as Anise continued to stride confidently towards the outskirts of the aerodrome where the tramp freighters and personal vehicles not important enough to be granted a space in the central aerodrome docked between journeys. The docking bays here were much smaller, on a scale of architecture that didn't immediately short-circuit the human brain. The *Howling Banshee* was in Bay 72 and Anise spared no time hesitating as she strode confidently up to the ship.

Like most pirate vessels the *Banshee* was designed for speed and stealth rather than cargo capacity or range. The modus operandi was to lie in wait for merchants in highly-trafficked channels, strike at targets of opportunity, and disappear before the authorities could respond. In an open port such as Aelelea the *Banshee* kept her guns hidden belowdecks and flew a flag of convenience. While the authorities might suspect any number of things wrong with the ship, as long as they couldn't *prove* conclusively they were pirates the *Banshee* was free to come and go as she pleased.

The *Banshee* looked like a normal short-distance hauler, not designed to ascend to the truly dangerous heights of the aether. The wooden hull of the ship was slung beneath the gas bag, rather than integrated like a dirigible, the two halves connected with great steel cables that would hold against even the worst weather. Anise didn't wait for permission from Jack or his crew and ascended the gangplank.

The entire crew were assembled on the deck and a handful gave catcalls as Anise boarded, although they were quickly silenced by their comrades. Like Jack, all of them had some sort of oxygen mask slung on their chest or around their neck and a blade at their belt. They were dressed practically but somewhat shabbily, as though the crew had clearly experienced hard times recently.

"Captain, this isn't Heliotrope," one of the pirates, a woman dressed in various shades of red and black, said.

"No, Crowley, Heliotrope is still a frog for the moment. We've been asked to fetch something from Hy-Brasil first. This is Anise, she's one of the Learned and she's decided to supervise. Do not antagonize her or I'll throw you over the rail myself." A couple of crew members had guilty looks on their faces and tried to shuffle further back into the crowd. "Well, come on, make ready to cast off. We've got work to do and we're burning daylight."

"Aye aye, Captain!" Crowley turned to the crew, shouting orders that made no sense to Anise whatsoever but had the crew leaping into action. Some of them went scurrying up the rigging to make adjustments to the ship's gasbag, while others started throwing off the mooring lines. Within a matter of minutes the ship started lifting into the air and the deck started to vibrate beneath them as the engines came to life. "Helm, are you ready to take us out?" Crowley asked.

"Aye aye, ma'am!"

"Take us up ahead slow, Helm. Mr. Opizzi, do you have contact with the tower?"

"Aye, ma'am, they're putting us into the pattern now."

Anise took a seat near the ship's aft rail and watched as the city of Aelelea came into bird's eye view. Captain Green stood like a monument on the *Banshee's* quarterdeck, projecting an aura of calm confidence to his crew, but Anise was skilled enough at illusions to recognize it was all projection on Jack's part. The subtle way his knees were locked a little too tightly and how his left hand kept clutching the hilt of his cutlass (when it wasn't nervously rubbing the pocket carrying Heliotrope's wooden box) gave him away. As simple as this quest might seem, it was obvious Jack wasn't so sure it would end well.

The *Banshee* worked her way into the traffic departing the city. In front of them was a great fat dirigible merchantman and behind was one of those great biological ships, an aether whale that soared through the sky as easily as its kin swam through the seas, with a sort of howdah perched on its back. Soon they received a green flag from the aerodrome's tower and the ship's engines roared as the *Banshee* climbed into the sky, everyone leaning forwards as the deck tilted backwards. Just when Anise was worried they would tumble out of their seat and be saved only by their wings, the *Banshee* leveled out and the quartermaster steered the ship towards one of the many portals that shimmered above Aelelea.

As the city between worlds, Aelelea stood at a point where the boundaries between universes were thin, rubbing up against each other much as tectonic plates scraped against each other along a fault line. And much like fault lines, great energy could be released in reality-shattering quakes. The very first portals between worlds had been ripped opened in the aftershocks of these quakes; Aelelea had been destroyed and rebuilt half a dozen times in their wake. Some portals were small, only a single person able to pass through at a time. Others were so large that an entire fleet of ships could sail side by side. The portals were the lifeblood of Aelelea. The Learned, as well as a significant chunk of Aelelea's civil service, helped manage the quakes and keep reality from fraying any further than it already had.

Their destination was a great white portal, its position

designated by a tower with two white flags marked with black exes. Unless you were aligned perfectly with the portal's position, it remained invisible to the naked eye. The ship was carefully nudged into position with the most delicate of adjustments of the wheel, and once Jack was satisfied his vessel was aligned properly and a wall of light shimmered in front of them, he gave the order. "All ahead full, all hands prepare for jump." The wind whipped past them and the ship's prow pierced the wall of the portal, disappearing to the other side.

Anise had never enjoyed portal travel. It always seemed to make their stomach do somersaults whenever they stepped from one world to another. Upon becoming a Learned they had been content to limit their life mostly to Aelelea, where the magic and people of a hundred worlds gathered together in a tremendous creole. But they could not pass up the opportunity to see a wonder such as Hy-Brasil and for that they were willing to suffer a little discomfort.

When they emerged on the other side of the portal, Anise felt about as green as their dress and it took several deep breaths before they felt their stomach settle once again. The skies were filled with clouds, obstructing the horizon in all directions. Only very brief breaks gave any indication of the direction of the sun overhead. If there was land below, Anise was unable to find it.

"Navigation, where are we?" Crowley barked. A woman Anise could only conclude was their navigator pulled out a series of instruments, including the ubiquitous sextant and compass, but also a small crystal pendant on a silver chain which she waved over the compass several times. After a series of calculations the navigator finally looked up.

"It looks like we're in luck today. Hy-Brasil is fifteen knots away, two points aft of the port beam."

"Bring her about, Helm." Jack's order was met with a chorus of ayes as the quartermaster brought the ship about to the left. The navigator kept a careful eye on her instruments until the pendant was swinging directly in line with the ship.

"Hy-Brasil, dead ahead!" she cried and the quartermaster stopped the great wheel, putting the *Banshee* back into trim. The navigator started taking other measurements, the purpose of which was dreadfully opaque to Anise. They walked up to Jack and tugged on his sleeve, a question in their mind.

"What did she mean by we're in luck? Isn't Hy-Brasil in the same place every day?"

Jack let out a chuckle. "Ah, that's the trouble with navigating the Sea of Clouds. You seriously didn't expect islands that flew in the sky to stay where they're put, did you?" He nodded towards the navigator who was in close consultation with the helmsman. "Sailing the Sea of Clouds is basically impossible without a crystal pendant since charts are impossible to make. If you know where you're going you can get relative heading and a rough estimate of distance, but without that you could sail the skies forever and never run into another soul. There are legends of ghost ships that still ply the aether, crewed only by the desiccated remains of their starved and dehydrated crews."

"They're true though," Crowley protested, looking up from her watch on the crew. "I've seen a ghost ship myself, ten years past."

"Impossible," Jack said. "Nothing but bedtime stories to scare greenhorn sailors from setting out across the Clouds without a proper navigator."

"Just because you haven't seen it with your own two eyes doesn't mean you can deny—"

"I haven't seen it with my own two eyes nor have I read about it nor heard in any of the many, many taverns I've frequented. And if someone *really* found a ghost ship you'd think they'd keep quiet about it?"

"I'm telling you now!"

Anise tuned out the argument between the captain and his first mate. They had to admit, the Sea of Clouds sure was lacking when it came to scenery. The clouds were all very fluffy and very impressive, but they'd already grown tired of looking at the same homogeneous skyscape after the first few minutes of sailing. "How long will it take us to travel the fifteen knots?" they asked the quartermaster.

"About an hour, m', more or less. Depends on if we catch the weather gauge." He turned the wheel slightly to the left at the prodding of the navigator. "You'll get the best view from up on the prow. Assuming you don't want to climb the gasbag."

Anise thanked the quartermaster and walked across the *Banshee*'s deck, adjusting their balance as the vessel occasionally pitched underneath them. The view from the prow wasn't really much better, but Anise felt slightly less in the way than they had on the quarterdeck. They decided to spend the time practicing small magics instead; it never hurt to keep even the most routine of skills sharp. They wove a small illusion, a bird in bright hues of scarlet and yellow that they sent flitting through the ship's rigging. It took a deft hand to control the illusion and keep it from dissolving or starting to look unnatural and was good practice.

Before they knew it, Anise heard the one of the crew from atop the gasbag shout "Land ahead!" Anise dismissed the illusion and turned back towards the ship's prow. Initially there was nothing to see, just another bank of clouds, but the island appeared from between two banks of fluffy towering cumulus clouds. It bore a passing resemblance to the drawing that Arty had shown them, although the forests carpeting the island were now long gone, replaced by collection of ramshackle buildings that had been built higgledy-piggledy on the gentle mountain slopes. Much like Aelelea it was a melange of architectural styles, with wooden cabins and bamboo pagodas sharing space with thatch houses. Countless mooring towers and cantilevered gantries allowed an armada of ships to dock.

And what an armada! Every possible ship that sailed the skies was guaranteed to be present at the docks of Hy-Brasil. Small cruisers and interceptors with gas bags, like the *Banshee*. Ships slung under the bellies or mounted on the backs of sleek cetaceans that swam the skies of a hundred worlds, and not the great lumbering beasts favored by merchants; these were the deadly sky orcas who were as swift as lightning and relished a good hunt as much as their human companions.

Anise spied one ship that seemed to be made of living wood, held aloft by great green leafy sails and which thrummed with a deep magic. And everywhere, absolutely everywhere were the ships the Artificer had shown them: Sleek craft that didn't have any obvious means of support but nonetheless remained in the sky. Two of these craft were approaching the *Banshee* and one ran up a series of colored flags. "Mr. Opizzi, they're asking for the recognition signal!" Crowley barked.

"Give me a minute," Opizzi replied as he ran to the flag locker and started running a series of colored flags up a signal mast. The very last one was larger than the others, a black rectangle with a traditional skull and crossbones located in the center. Whatever this message said, and Anise could only guess, it seemed to satisfy the patrolling craft, who let the *Banshee* advance without any further comment.

"Captain, where do you want us to set down?" the quartermaster asked, slowing the ship as they entered the complex and chaotic traffic pattern of the sky around Hy-Brasil. If there was a central tower that was organizing all this traffic, Anise certainly didn't see it.

"Take us to Lady Rodriguez's dock."

"Aye aye, Captain." The *Banshee* dipped towards the island and headed towards a tidy-looking dock on one of the lower levels of the island. A series of cable stays and steel trusses helped keep the dock suspended off the edge of the island, and Anise could see two other vessels docked there. One was a small, personal craft good for little more than short jaunts around the island. It was built in the same style as the other Heart-powered ships so Anise could only assume this one had the same means of propulsion. The other was a medium-sized dirigible in the same class as the *Banshee* with a snarling tiger painted across its envelope.

"That'll be Pearson's *Tiger*. Didn't realize he was still running to Hy-Brasil," Jack said.

"He's worked with the Artificer before. You anticipating a problem?" Crowley asked.

"No. No, I don't imagine so. I'm sure if we don't go around poking into his business he'll repay us the same courtesy."

The *Banshee* slowed to a crawling pace as settled into the dock. Already several dockhands were standing by with hawsers and flung them to the *Banshee*'s crew as the ship came alongside. There was hardly even a bump as the *Banshee* finally came to a rest. The crew were huddled excitedly around the gangway as it slammed down on the dock and were ready to run down it when a shout from Crowley stopped them in their tracks.

"All right," Jack said when the crew was more or less paying attention. "Nobody's leaving the ship while we're in port." This was met by a chorus of groans and curses from the crew. "We're spending a day here at the most and I haven't got time to round you all out of every tavern and bawdy house on the Island. So you're all staying on board while I take care of business. Crowley's in charge while I'm gone. Winslow, Snapp, you're with me. Anise I can't really tell you what you can or can't do so you're welcome to come along but we're leaving within the day."

"All right, you all heard the captain. Get the rigging in order. I want us ready to lift at a moment's notice!" Crowley barked some more orders at the crew as Jack headed down the gangplank. Two heavily-armed men who probably were in the dictionary next to the word "enforcer" followed without a further comment. Anise decided the risk of getting left behind in Hy-Brasil was well worth whatever they was going to find out from this particular adventure and joined them.

As they stepped onto the dock, Anise saw a tall woman storming towards them. And storm was the appropriate word, Anise was fairly sure they had seen thunderclouds with less menace than the approach of her large, black hat and swinging parasol. Jack turned and greeted her with an insincerely cheerful, "Audrey! How have you—" at which point Jack's salutation was cut short because the woman had whacked him in the stomach with her parasol.

Jack bent over in pain and let forth a stream of curses only to be interrupted once again as the woman beat Jack again with the parasol. She would have kept going if Snapp and Winslow had not intervened, grabbing her makeshift weapon and managing to wrest it out of her hands. "You've got a lot of goddamn nerve coming to my dock after that stunt you pulled! *And* after what Heliotrope did to the Artificer. Arty was finally starting to feel at home there, and she goes and poisons the well! Where is she, the bewinged bitch? Is that her?" The woman pointed at Anise and stopped her assault on Jack switch targets. "Listen here, you heartless, lying, thrice-cursed—"

"I'm afraid you have me at an advantage," Anise explained, their hands raised in self-defense. "My name is Anise, I'm a good friend of Arty and I'm here to help Jack finish a favor he owes Arty."

"Oh, well if that's the case I sincerely apologize. I'm Lady Audrey Rodriguez, I own this dock." Audrey gave Anise a welcoming smile and offered her hand in greeting. "It's a pleasure to meet you, Anise. The Artificer mentioned you in one of their letters and they only had nice things to say. However this *scum*," she jerked her head towards Jack and his subordinates, "can take themselves off with the rest of the garbage."

"I have a chit and you have to honor it," Jack said, finally upright and slightly recovered from his encounter with the parasol. He rummaged in his pockets and pulled out a slip of red paper, waving it towards Audrey. "I have a chit from your own hand giving me twenty-four hours of berthing space because we overpaid the last time we were here and you couldn't give me a refund."

Audrey took the proffered paper and looked it over. "If this wasn't enchanted I'd rip it up right now and tell you to shove off. Fine. You have twenty-four hours at my dock but one minute over and I'm impounding your rat-infested ship and throwing your entire crew off." Audrey took out a pen from a pouch on her belt and made a mark on the paper which glowed briefly with red light and then faded, before she handed it back to Jack.

"Thank you, Audrey!" Jack called to her retreating back. "All right, let's make this quick. We've got to locate the Heart, get a piece, and get back out before that woman takes my ship. Or we meet anyone else who thinks they owe us a grudge."

"I'm definitely noticing a theme where people seem to want you dead," Anise said. "Or at the very least injured."

"Not *everyone* feels that way about me," Jack protested. "I have quite a few friends." They were passing near a building at the end of the dock labeled "OFFICE" and the door slammed open, revealing a tall, bearded man with a sword in one hand.

"YOU!" the man shouted.

"I just can't seem to find any right now! Everyone scatter!" Jack ran off into the streets of Hy-Brasil, one hand on his sword, the other clutching his hat. Snapp and Winslow split in opposite directions, leaving a string of overturned carts and curses in their wake. The man with the sword wasted no time deciding which person to chase and continued after Jack, uttering promises of what he was going to do with Jack's skin when he finally caught him.

Anise was left wondering where they would meet the pirates again. "I'm starting to think Heliotrope deserved to get turned into a frog after all," they said.

* * *

It wasn't terribly difficult for Anise to find Jack afterwards,;tracking spells were fairly simple magic, and while a conventional search might have been like seeking the proverbial needle in a haystack, it was the work of moments to find the pub where Jack and his compatriots had reassembled. Which was a good thing because based on their very limited survey, Anise suspected Hy-Brasil was almost forty percent pub by volume. "That was a very interesting encounter," Anise said, sitting down at the rickety table. They winced at the condition of the pewter tankards on the table and elected not to order. "Any other old friends we need to worry about you running into?"

Somewhere between the dock and here Jack had found a plain gray cloak to cover his trademark green outfit and a black very wide-brimmed hat to help hide his face. "As long as we move fast, I think we'll be able to avoid any further entanglements."

"We have twenty-two hours on the clock, boss," one of the enforcers said. Whether it was Winslow or Snapp Anise couldn't tell, they had trouble keeping the two apart. "Where are we going to find the Heart anyway?"

Jack shushed his crew member with a wave of his hand and looked around the pub carefully before leaning over the table and gesturing for everyone to draw closer. "Just because a great many people know about the Heart doesn't mean it's not *supposed* to be a secret." Jack pulled a cloth map out from one of the many, many pockets his outfit seemed to have. It was a rough outline of Hy-Brasil that showed the island sliced in cross-section. "The island itself was discovered by accident nearly two hundred years ago. A smuggler on the Sea of Clouds was trying to hide from the authorities and stumbled onto its shores. She found out it was riddled with caves, which seemed like an ideal hiding spot from the authorities, and set up a small smugglers' base on the island. More importantly she took a handful of crystals from the caves when she left, which meant she was able to actually find the island again."

"The crystal pendant, of course!" Anise said. "Thaumaturgic entanglement! The crystal remembers where it's from, which means—"

"Yes yes, like calls to like, we all know," Jack said, taking control of the conversation again. The Learned could derail an entire conversation when a a particularly interesting subject came up. "But it wasn't after a good fifty years of exploring and charting the caverns of Hy-Brasil that they finally found the Heart." Jack pointed towards a chamber in the center of the island which was hatched in lines resembling radiating light. "So all we need to do is sneak into the caverns, find our way to the Heart Chamber, score off a piece of the Heart, find our way back out, and quietly leave. *And* we have tools!" Jack produced a small rock hammer and a chisel which he had somehow secreted on his person as well.

"That's all well and good, captain," Winslow said, or maybe it was Snapp, "but the caves stretch on for miles and twist back around on themselves. We could spend *weeks* trying to find our way to the Heart and if we leave a ball of string to find our way back out we're *guaranteed* to have some damn fool stumble across it sooner or later."

"And we've only got," Snapp, or perhaps Winslow, looked at his pocket watch, "Twenty-three hours and fifteen minutes left."

"What exactly is it that makes the Heart distinct from other parts of the island?" Anise asked, the glimmerings of an idea in their mind that needed details to flesh it out. "What special quality makes the Heart the Heart?"

"The Heart is what keeps Hy-Brasil flying," Jack explained. "Most of the island is ordinary rock which if you tossed it into the Sea of Clouds would fall down to nobody knows where. Pieces of the Heart, though, are able to fly *and* can carry a certain amount of weight, which is why they're so valuable for airships. You *do* have to get the magic right, because if you don't calibrate the energies properly your ship will fall right out of the sky. That's why I always stick to gas bags, they come with their own risks but—"

"What if I just target the strongest source of magic and we try to find it from there?" Anise interrupted. The pirates looked at them blankly.

"You can do that?" Snapp asked.

"Do y'all not do basic magic?" Anise asked, looking from one confused pirate to the other. "It's a dead simple detection spell."

"Most people…can't do magic?" Jack offered as a hesitant explanation. "I mean, our navigator can do some basic wayfinding charms but most of what you do" he gestured vaguely at Anise, "is beyond us."

"Well, it's a good thing for you I decided to tag along then, isn't it?"

* * *

The streets of Hy-Brasil never seemed to be deserted, which made blending in all the easier for the quartet. There also seemed to be an unspoken code in Hy-Brasil that everyone scrupulously avoided looking at anyone else's business which made all manner of clandestine business easier to transact. You certainly couldn't follow everyone acting suspiciously when literally *everyone* was acting suspiciously. But Anise would have felt slightly better if the pirates skulking behind them just walked normally. Jack's directions took them down a small alley to their right and at the end they were rewarded with a wooden cellar door. With no obvious lock or warding spell, Anise went ahead and pulled it open, revealing a series of steps leading down into the island.

Once they stepped inside Anise summoned a small ball of golden light to illuminate the cellar. It looked like most ordinary cellars, with bins full of staple root vegetables and the barrels and jars that most people kept in their domestic cellars. But hidden behind one of the barrels was a passage that led further into the mountain. "Come on, this way," Anise said as the pirates managed to trip over both their cutlasses and their attempts to look inconspicuous. Anise merely rolled their eyes and headed down the tunnel.

Very quickly the finished stonework of the cellar gave way to the living rock of the cave. Anise stopped and began working on their tracking spell, which required careful calibration. It would have been simplicity itself to latch onto the most powerful source of magic and get a direction on it, but Anise was certain they would have ended up in front of a stone wall as the spell pulled them insistently towards the center of the island and no further information on how to get there. It took a considerably more complicated spell to actually analyze the terrain from here to there and give you the best way to navigate. Fortunately, Anise had been rapidly expanding their repertoire beyond illusions in the six months since the bank heist.

Anise closed their eyes and extended their magical senses. At first there was an absolute riot of magic from half a hundred practitioners in every color of the rainbow, but they started filtering out any magic that didn't *yearn* to fly. That narrowed the field considerably to just a few shades. Anything which was the only example of its color Anise ruled out out immediately, and they were left with only sources of deep blueish-gray and a dark scarlet. When Anise "touched" the deep gray they heard a song made of eerie whistles and moans made by no human throat. It took a moment but then a flash of insight, the sky whales! Beautiful, but not what they were looking for.

Anise turned their attention to the scarlet and tried to sort the sources in their head. There were dozens if not hundreds of sources of that particular shade of magic. They concentrated and filtered out anything smaller than ten kilograms, which should remove anything used to power a ship. That still left three major sources of magic and Anise frowned. Two were well above them and while it was *possible* those sources were ships, the ships themselves would have been behemothic dreadnoughts that Anise couldn't have missed when they arrived. It was only the third source, deep below them, which convinced Anise they had found the magical signature of the Heart. Anise let the magic find its path, and then led the pirates into the depths below

At every turning point in the cave system, Anise took a moment to leave a magic mark, really a small illusion of an arrow in their favorite forest green to let them know the way back out. Undaunted by the twists and turns in the cave system, Anise headed deeper into the mountain as the pirates followed at their sneaking pace.

"You know you can really cut that out now," Anise said after they had caught the pirates trying to not look suspicious for the umpteenth time. "There's nobody down here to see us and if we do run into someone they're probably going to be suspicious as to why we're down here in the first place anyway. Your creeping about with catlike tread is getting downright silly."

"It's the principle of the thing though," Jack explained. "We're pirates, we're on a secret mission, we have to at least *act* like we're trying to not get discovered."

"Well then act like you belong here! That's what we did when we…Oh my." Anise's rant was cut off by the next cavern chamber which they entered. So far the cave had not been terribly interesting — well, that was a bit of lie because a dedicated caver or geologist would have found the caves inside Hy-Brasil absolutely fascinating. But Anise and the pirates were neither spelunkers nor scientists so most of the features inside the cave were wasted on them, but the next chamber would take almost everyone's breath away. Amethyst crystals, ranging in size from Anise's smallest finger to as large as Jack's fist grew from almost every surface. The only part of the cave not covered with the purple crystals was a path leading from one end of the room to the other.

The crystals themselves glowed with a soft purple light, making Anise's light spell utterly unnecessary. Anise had no head for numbers but this room was big enough that the *Banshee* probably could have fit inside; it would have been a tight squeeze, but you could do it. "Jack, give me your rock hammer," Anise said, the pirate was too overwhelmed by the crystals to argue and obediently relinquished his tool. Anise bent over and carefully chipped at a finger-sized crystal. As soon as it was disconnected from the cavern the crystal ceased to glow, becoming for all intents and purposes an ordinary piece of amethyst. Anise secreted the crystal into their pocket and returned the rock hammer to Jack. "Come on, we should be fairly close now."

The next chamber was no less interesting because it was

filled with great slabs of obsidian. Anise felt their illumination spell struggle and flicker as the light seemed to get sucked into the obsidian. Anise considered stopping to get a sample of the rock but the strain on their spell was worrying so they hurried the pirates through a narrow crack into the next chamber.

"Dionysus's balls, would you look at that!" Jack said when they finally made their way through the cave wall. If the chamber with the amethysts had been large, this one was truly gargantuan. Anise's light, renewed to brightness due to the absence of the obsidian, was still barely enough to light even the closest corners of this room. Somewhere far above them, although they had no idea where, was presumably the cave ceiling. The center of the room was taken up by a truly massive irregularly-shaped blood-red stone. Even if its size and rich color weren't enough to attract attention, the fact that it was hovering at least two meters off the floor of the cave would cue even the most oblivious observer that this rock was *magic*. "The Heart of Hy-Brasil."

Anise was almost overwhelmed by the sheer amount of magic they could sense in the room. "The obsidian in the last room must act like a sort of dampener, absorbing the magic to keep it from overwhelming everything. Oh, I wish Arty and Teal were here, they're so much better at the analysis side than I am."

"So I guess we just chip off a part of the Heart then? Anybody see a way up there?" They looked around the cavern but it was devoid of any furniture which could have been pressed into service as a makeshift ladder. The pirates were about to start forming a human pyramid with Jack perched precariously on top of Winslow and Snapp when Anise sighed.

"All right, fine, I'll do it," Anise said, taking the rock hammer from Jack's hands and flying up to get a good look at the Heart. The thing Anise noticed first was how warm the Heart felt, like it truly was alive and radiating body heat; if Anise spent too long up here, they'd start sweating through their gown in a matter of moments. The Heart's magic tingled against their skin and Anise briefly wondered what long-term exposure to the Heart might do to a person. They decided it was probably best to work quickly and leave any hypothetical questions to the Artificer when they next spoke.

The Heart was covered in scars where pieces of the rock had obviously been chipped away by other people. Anise looked for a spot that would be relatively easy to break off and found a crack running through part of the stone. Anise hovered closer and ran their fingers over the crack. It seemed to run deep into the Heart, as if the stone had been placed under quite a lot of strain. Anise carefully lined up the rock hammer a few centimeters away from the crack, tapped the rock gently with the sharp end of the hammer, then raised it and gave the rock a good strike. The steel of the hammer sang as it struck the Heart and a palm-sized fragment chipped off, flying into the air. Anise managed to snag it before it tumbled to the cave floor. The stone felt warm in their hand, like it was alive, but the warmth as well as the red glow of the stone quickly dissipated. In a matter of moments it was nothing more than a very ordinary-looking stone. "All right, I've got what we came for!"

"That's great! Because we've got something of a development down here!" Jack said.

Anise looked down and found the pirates standing back-to-back with their weapons drawn. Surrounding them were a dozen people led by the bearded man who had pursued Jack from the dock. "You know, I had a bad opinion of you before, Jack, but I didn't expect you to stoop so low as to steal a piece of the Heart. But I suppose if the Autumn Court tells you to jump, you do it with a smile on your lips."

"Ain't any affair of the Autumn Court," Jack said, his eyes darting back and forth among the opponents surrounding him. Anise could practically hear his brain calculating the odds.

"That's true," Anise said helpfully from above the brewing fight. "I'm actually Learned, we're doing this as a favor to the Artificer."

"I greatly respect the Artificer," Pearson said. "Never sat right with me, them getting exiled like that, and I've half a mind to flay Heliotrope alive myself. But we caught you in the act and I can always use reward money. Running a ship ain't cheap, as I'm sure you know. Now are you going to come quietly—" Pearson never got the chance to finish that sentence as Jack lunged with his cutlass and put Pearson on the defensive. With a roar Pearson's crew charged forward and it looked for a moment like the trio of pirates would be overwhelmed. However, it was obvious that Jack's crew had extensive experience at being outnumbered and they managed to fend off their numerically superior foe.

"Anise, if you'd like to help, now would be the time!" Jack shouted as he parried one sword and wrenched an axe from an another opponent's hand.

"What do you expect me to do?" Anise dodged as one of Pearson's crew fired a pistol in their direction. They felt the bullet whiz by their wing and strike the stone ceiling far above them.

"You're a magic user! You could cast a fireball or something!"

"I'm not that sort of magic user! I specialize in illusions! If you wanted somebody who could sling fireballs you should have asked Teal for help! Although…" Anise frowned as they concentrated. They had an idea but it was going to take a lot of finesse to do it properly. They tugged on threads of magic and started weaving them together into an incredibly tight, dense mesh. Anise's hands blurred with motion and when they finished one enchantment they moved to another until they created twelve different spheres of darkness and quickly placed them over the heads of Pearson and his crew; the pirates now looked like they were wearing old timey astronaut fishbowl helmets of darkest night. This was met with shouts of dismay and anger from the attackers. Jack and his two crewmates were about to get some of their own back but Anise was already flying towards the exit.

"Jack, we don't have time for this. I can barely keep the illusions in place as it is." One of Pearson's crew had taken the simple expedient of dropping to the floor and had managed to escape the sphere of conjured darkness long enough to give either Snapp or Winslow some trouble before Anise was able to situate the black bubble back over their head. "Let's *GO*." Anise didn't bother to look back as they fled from the Heart's chamber and into the room filled with obsidian. Anise felt their magic flicker and weaken and they had to land back on the ground to maintain enough concentration and keep the illusion going. About halfway through the chamber Anise felt their illusion finally break and there were the distant shouts of Pearson's crew realizing they could see again.

"Can you bring the cave down on them or something?" Jack asked as he and his crew ran to keep up with Anise.

"What? No. Don't be ridiculous," Anise scoffed.

"Rock just sucks up magic and it wouldn't work?" he guessed.

"No, it's just well out of my capabilities. The Jade Duke could have done it when he still had power. Although you might not end up on the same side of the rock as him." They had entered the amethyst chamber now and were quickly navigating the plethora of violet crystals. The light they gave off now seemed to be angry, as if the island itself was aware of what was happening. Multiple times Anise and the pirates had to shift direction as jagged spikes of crystal suddenly shot up in their path, threatening to impale them. It was only thanks to Anise's magical talents and the pirates' honed reflexes that they escaped at all.

From there it was a simple matter of following Anise's magic symbols back to the surface. No matter how fast they ran or how convoluted their path seemed to get, they could hear the sounds of dogged pursuit behind them. "What exactly did you do to piss off this Pearson fellow?"

"You mean aside from steal a piece of the Heart?" Jack asked in a moment where he still had breath. "Well, you'd have to ask Heliotrope and the Artificer for the whole story." There was the sound of someone excitedly shouting that they'd picked up the trail behind them and Jack somehow managed to find more reserves of energy. "But maybe when we're not being chased!"

Finally they emerged, blinking, into the sunlight. "Everyone split up, it'll be easier for us to escape individually than as a group. We'll rendezvous at the *Banshee*," Jack said, not even looking back as he ran down and alley and jumped over a pile of crates. Apparently this was a standard strategy for the pirates as Snapp and Winslow took off in different directions, one scaling a building by scurrying up a drainpipe, one disappearing into a convenient crowd of market-goers. Anise shrugged their shoulders and merely took to the sky, making a beeline for Lady Rodriguez's dock.

If anyone took notice of Anise's flight across Hy-Brasil, they didn't do much about it. A handful of fae and other bewinged humanoids of various descriptions were going about their business so it certainly wasn't an unusual occurrence. As they approached the dock, however, Anise was unsurprised to discover other members of Pearson's crew had established a cordon across the entry to the berth where the *Banshee* was docked. Crowley and the rest of the *Banshee's* crew looked down from the deck, clearly agitated by this most recent development. Anise spotted Jack lurking behind a stack of crates that were conveniently placed everywhere in Hy-Brasil and they landed behind him.

"You have any brilliant ideas?" Jack asked as Anise walked up.

"Aren't you supposed to be this brilliant pirate captain? I haven't heard you come up with one plan this entire time."

"Heliotrope usually has the clever plans," Jack admitted, looking back at twenty or so armed crew who stood between them and the *Banshee's* gangplank. "I'm here to look dashing and wield a sword."

"Well, a *smart* plan," Anise said, "would make use of our particular strengths and assets. What is the likelihood that Pearson's crew would chase after an illusion of you?"

"Unlikely," Jack admitted. "They're highly disciplined. Pearson takes pride in how well-trained they are. Could you do something like a spell of invisibility?"

"Invisibility is hard. Making us look like something else which is supposed to be there is much easier. Shame there aren't any more ships on this dock, we could really use someone who looks like they're supposed to be here." At that moment both Snapp and Winslow, who it seemed had rendezvoused somewhere else, appeared at the end of the dock. One of the sentries gave a cry and all of Pearson's crew advanced on the two pirates, weapons drawn.

"Damn, that's torn it," Jack said as the two enforcers drew their own blades, making it clear they intended to fight their way through overwhelming odds. He was about to jump from cover and join his wayward crewmates when Anise tapped him on the shoulder.

"Jack, should they be running out a cannon?"

"Who, the *Tiger*?"

"No, your crew." Anise pointed towards the *Banshee* and one of the gun ports had opened, revealing a cannon aimed in the general direction of the impending melee.

"Crew, load grapeshot and stand by to fire!" Crowley shouted in a voice meant to be heard over the roar of combat and which all of Pearson's crew heard in perfect clarity. Crowley gave the order to fire and everyone scrambled for cover, Jack tackling Anise to the ground as the loud boom of the cannon sounded and something whizzed overhead. Wood snapped and glass shattered.

Anise pushed Jack off of them and stood up. The damage was relatively slight, all things considered. Everyone had found cover behind something sturdy enough to protect them from the iron projectiles, although Lady Rodriguez's personal skiff would need some repairs before it was ready to fly again. Jacks, Snapp, and Winslow wasted no time in recovering and sprinted towards the gangplank, stumbling the last few feet to the relative safety of the *Banshee*. Anise flew after them in just as much of a hurry.

"Crowley, are you insane?" Jack asked just as Crowley authorized another whiff of grapeshot in the general direction of their pursuers. "You've broken the truce!" Emphasizing this point was an extremely angry Rodriguez emerging from her office, revolver in hand, as she stormed towards the *Banshee* hurriedly casting off from the dock. Anise couldn't hear what Rodriguez was saying, but she looked murderous as she leveled her pistol and fired. The bullets thudded into the *Banshee's* hull, which was a bit of an anticlimax, but Rodriguez was still coming towards them and she was reloading.

"What was I supposed to do? Let the three of you get captured by Pearson? Besides, he broke the truce first. And it's too late to be worrying about truces now," Crowley snapped, then turned to the rest of the crew. "Run out the cannons, load with grapeshot!"

"Belay that!" Jack countermanded. "Last thing I need is this escalating into a full-fledged war."

"Lines away, captain!" shouted a crewwoman. The *Banshee* bobbed slightly in the air, drifting slowly away from the dock.

"Where are our engines?" Jack asked, running up to the quarterdeck and hauling on the great ship's wheel himself.

"Still firing up," Crowley said.

"You want to explain to me why you ran the cannons out but didn't think to get the engines ready?" The *Banshee* continued to drift serenely, pushed by the wind away from the dock at an agonizingly slow pace.

"I ordered them to start, but they said something about the aether not being right for it." Jack did not take this answer well and based on his facial expression was ready to strangle Crowley. "Listen, I did my job, getting mad at me isn't going to solve it."

"Your job was to keep everything under control, not start a war with the entirety of Hy-Brasil!" Jack dashed down into the hold and the sounds of shouted explanations and copious swearing that only an air-pirate could muster floated up, muffled by the wood deck.

"I don't suppose there's anything you could do to help?" Crowley asked, turning to Anise. "Ideally give us a fair wind?"

"Once again, outside my specialization, but I'll see what I can do." Anise sighed, stepping to the rail. Rodriguez and Pearson's crew had reemerged from cover and were making various attempts at pursuit. Rodriguez and a handful of people were examining the skiff, attempting to jury-rig repairs and get it airborne again. The rest of Pearson's crew were hurriedly trying to get the tiger-painted dirigible into the air.

Anise focused on a patch of sky behind the *Banshee* not visible to the people on the dock and started weaving strands of light. Strand by strand, Anise put them together into the shape of a great green dragon with golden wings. They had their illusion flap its wings and do a few shallow dives as a test. Satisfied that it looked more or less convincing Anise brought it around the stern of the *Banshee* and sent the dragon flying towards the dock.

The hard part about illusions wasn't creating a convincing image, plenty of mages nowhere even a tenth as talented as Anise could make an image convincing enough to trick casual inspection. The real skill, and this is where Anise really shined, was in making the illusions *real*. It was the sound of the dragon's wings as they passed through the air, it was that same air getting pushed down towards you as the dragon flew overhead. There were a thousand tiny details to make people really *think* that a dragon was flying overhead and Anise mastered them all.

The people on the dock scurried for cover once again as the dragon dove towards them. Anise had it let out a mighty roar and the people hurriedly fled dirigible. It seemed they did indeed have to rely on flammable gas to get that great airship flying. As the dragon started to wing into the air, it let out a great plume of orange flame that caused many people to shout in terror or dismay. Anise couldn't help but grin to themselves. This was definitely fun.

"That'll buy us some time for sure," Crowley said, clearly impressed by the results.

"They'll figure out pretty quick that's just an illusion, though," Anise said as the dragon lazily wheeled about and made another dive towards the dock. People were definitely going to notice when seasoned timber failed to catch on fire. Fortunately they felt the deck hum underneath them as the engines finally engaged and the *Banshee* started its flight from the island. Anise kept the illusion going for as long as they could, keeping their pursuers scattered and more concerned with imminent immolation, but when said fiery end failed to materialize and people began taking potshots at the dragon, Anise decided the illusion had run its course and dispelled it.

The *Banshee* had made good progress and Jack was back on the quarterdeck, but they were still within sight of the island and already many of the patrol craft were starting to turn in their direction. "All engines ahead full, get me everything you've got," Jack said into a speaking tube. Anise didn't hear the response, but the hum of the engines entered a higher register and the deck vibrated worryingly beneath them. He and Crowley looked back towards Hy-Brasil. Pearson's *Tiger* was finally getting underway, although the large dirigible was slow in its movements as it carefully cast off from the dock. More worryingly were the smaller craft rapidly drawing closer.

Suddenly flashes of light appeared on the decks of the leading craft. "They're firing on us! Run out the guns!" Jack shouted as shells whizzed past the *Banshee*. Any crew that could be spared from the *Banshee's* flight hurried to open hatches. Several deck guns emerged from the hatches and the crew hurried readied to fire.

Anise turned their attention to their pursuers and was struck at the sight of the ugly, gray projectiles arcing through the air. Then gravity overcame their momentum and they plummeted to the endless depths below. "At least they don't seem to be able to hit us," they said.

"They're just finding the range," Jack said, frowning worriedly as the guns of their pursuers flashed again. "It's a race for all of us now. If we get far enough away they won't be able to keep up the pursuit. The question is can we get away before they bracket us." The shells were much closer this time, whizzing past the hull of the *Banshee* and speeding forward before dropping. "There it is. Hard to port! All guns, prepare to fire!"

The *Banshee* groaned as she turned. Anise had to grab onto the rail to keep themselves from slipping on the tilted deck but the gunners on the port side were sure-footed, swiveling their weapons about and doing whatever it was gunners did in combat situations. Anise saw the patrol craft break formation and scatter in response to the *Banshee's* broadside. Jack ordered the ship to turn to starboard and begin fleeing straight away from the enemy once again. The island was so distant now that Anise could cover it with their hand, and they felt their heart raise as the small craft broke off pursuit, turning back towards their base. This elation was short lived, however, as the great mass of the *Tiger* rose through the clouds.

"He can't possibly catch us, not with his mass," Crowley said. "The wind resistance alone…"

"Just has to wound us enough we can't go at top speed," Jack said. "He can outlast us in a long chase and he knows it. Navigation! How long till we reach the portal back to Aelelea?"

The navigator looked up from her instruments. "It's shifted at least ten knots, the aetheric winds are strong today. Starboard abeam of us." The quartermaster started turning the wheel to get the *Banshee* headed in the correct general direction. There was an explosion in the air directly ahead of them and the ship shuddered as it was sprinkled with shrapnel. One pirate screamed as they fell from the rigging, wounded, and disappeared into the clouds below.

"He knows where we're headed, the clever bastard," Jack said. "He'll try to herd us away from the portal and then get between us and it. If he can keep us here in the air he can wear us down, bring us back to Hy-Brasil." There was another series of explosions and the quartermaster swore as they tried to steer the ship out of the way. There was a ripping noise overhead as shrapnel bit into the canvas of the gas bag and the *Banshee* dipped worryingly. Pirates scrambled to patch the holes and keep their ship airborne.

"Crowley, can you get our guns firing back? At least ruin their aim?"

"No good, he's got heavier guns and he's got range on us. Best I can do is distract him a little." The gunners of the aft-most guns fired their weapons and some several hundred meters behind the *Banshee* two clouds of thick, red smoke spread from the burst shells. The winds spread the smoke widely and it looked pathetically thin against the Sea of Clouds.

"What if I made us disappear in the clouds?" Anise asked. "It'll work better if you can give us some clouds to take cover in first."

Jack scanned the sky and found a large cloud to the left. "Helm, hard to port and dive us into that cloud." The quartermaster merely answered aye and everyone grabbed onto a handhold as the ship tilted to port and dropped, the wind whipping through the rigging. As they entered the cloud visibility dropped to only a few feet, a white mist shrouding everything. They could still hear the sound of shells bursting as the *Tiger* tried to flush them from cover and the ship creaked in protest.

Anise acted quickly. A Learned more experienced with elements such as Teal would have simply pulled the cloud with them, ordering the water vapor to do as they commanded. Anise would once again have to rely upon their illusions, but with the benefit that they would be able to see *out* of this cloud. Carefully, they built a cloud around the *Banshee*, resisting the temptation to make it shaped like something memorable. That would be sure to attract attention so Anise settled for a nice, puffy, cotton ball. The sunlight dimmed as the illusion took shape, reflecting light back to give the appearance of a perfectly ordinary cloud.

"Cut the engines!" Anise advised as they put the finishing touches on their illusion.

"What, why?" Crowley asked.

"You ever see a cloud run contrary to the wind?" Jack asked, catching on to Anise's intent. "Cut the engines and run out the emergency sails." The crew scrambled to do as he ordered and the deck ceased to vibrate beneath them. Two spars were run out amidships and pirates hauled on ropes to set the sails. Soon the Banshee was pushed along solely by the wind. "Steady hand, helm, keep us following the wind."

"Aye-aye captain." Nobody dared to breathe as the *Banshee* slowly nosed her way out of the cloud bank. There was a quiet gasp from someone as the *Tiger* came into sight, barely two kilometers away from them and it was only a stern order from Jack that kept the crew from scurrying back to battle stations. The *Tiger* continued to fire into the cloud bank they had just left behind, trying to flush the *Banshee* out of hiding. Time slowed to a crawl as everyone waited to see if their ruse would fall apart, but the crew of the *Tiger* took no notice of the new cloud gently drifting away.

Over the course of an hour the *Banshee* slowly pulled away from their pursuers. They had to follow the winds, but the quartermaster was a deft enough hand to put them more or less in the general direction they wanted to go. Eventually the *Tiger* disappeared behind the innumerable clouds and Jack risked activating the engines to finish their journey to the portal. Within another half an hour the shimmering portal back to Aelelea was within sight and the *Banshee*'s return to the city between worlds was almost an anti-climax.

* * *

"Well you did it. You really managed to bring me a piece of the Heart." The Artificer looked up from the fragment of stone they were examining. "And here I thought you'd die in the attempt."

"You thought this was a suicide mission and you let me go with them?" Anise said, putting extra hysterics into their voice just to needle Arty. Arty's expression made it clear they were having none of that nonsense today.

"We've done our part of the bargain," Jack said, clearly ready for this entire stressful business to be over with. He carefully removed Heliotrope from her box and presented her to Arty. "Now hurry up and kiss my wife." Anise discreetly kicked Arty when it looked like they'd protest so Arty merely sighed and leaned forward. They screwed their eyes shut, clearly not wanting to think about kissing a poison dart frog, and planted a kiss right on Heliotrope's head. Arty shot back as soon as it was done, brushing their mouth with their hand.

Jack looked at Heliotrope, waiting for something dramatic to happen. "Did you do it right? Maybe you need to kiss her again?"

"Absolutely under no circumstances will I be—" The rest of Arty's argument was cut off as Heliotrope's frog body suddenly glowed a bright yellow-white. Shocked, Jack dropped her but she merely floated in the air, her body now nothing more than soft light, a silhouette rapidly transforming from frog to humanoid. There was a sudden flash of intense light, forcing everyone to close their eyes, and then Heliotrope was simply *there*. She was tall and willowy-thin, her skin a sort of soft violet-pink that you would see on flowers but rarely on humans, and stretching from her back were two great wings.

"I can't believe that actually worked," she said, looking at her hands in surprise. "I'll have to remember that for next time I curse someone, it's a delicious twist on an old classic."

"Yes, well, you can get the hell out of my house," Arty said, already making for their reference library. "This was *not* a pleasure. Do *not* feel free to come back anytime." Arty would have kept going but Anise had kicked them in the shin again and they muttered curses in a dead language.

"Heliotrope, I'm so happy you're back! I was so afraid I'd never see you again! I— Ow! What was that for?" Heliotrope had slapped Jack across the face and he had staggered back, more shocked than physically hurt.

"Frogs may not be good at hearing, but even in a wooden box I could hear you and that tart Crowley in the middle of the night. How long has that been going on?"

"Heliotrope, we talked about this. You were interested in that one gentleman of the court so we opened our relationship—"

"Which ended in me getting turned into a frog and you apparently taking up with whatever strumpet on your moon-forsaken boat which catches your fancy. If you think I want to stay married to you, you've got another thing coming."

"Out," Arty said, picking up a broom and pushing at both Jack and Heliotrope. "You two can squabble all you like, but do it *somewhere else*. Out."

"Oh, I haven't even *begun* with you, Arty!" Heliotrope's nostrils flared as a combination of Arty's pushing and Jack's pulling moved her towards the door. "I will make you rue the day that you ever crossed paths with me."

"You already did that. Out." Heliotrope would have continued her diatribe but she was already on the other side of the threshold and Arty slammed the steel door in her face. They sighed as they slammed the bolt home. "Try getting through iron that I've touched, you Fae bitch."

"Arty! Language."

"You aren't my parent. I should know, I buried them." Arty returned to the counter and looked at the piece of the Heart again. "Incredible. And you're sure it's genuine?"

"Broke it off from the Heart of Hy-Brasil myself," Anise said with pride. They added the amethyst crystal to the table as well. "*And* I got a navigation crystal so we can go back once things have calmed down."

"Impressive." Arty leaned back and crossed their arms, giving Anise an appraising look. "So y'all didn't bother to just go *buy* a piece of the Heart in the market?" The flabbergasted look on Anise's face told Arty all the information they needed to know. "No, I suppose not. Wouldn't have been Jack's way after all."

"You mean we went to all this trouble and effort of stealing a piece of the Heart, fighting Pearson, breaking the truce, hiding in clouds, and gods alone know what else—"

"Oh, you ran into Pearson, eh?"

"Yes!" Anise's teeth were gritted now. "Arty, you had better start explaining some things right now."

"All right, all right." Arty held up their hands placatingly. "Based on the fact I still have friends in Hy-Brasil I probably could have just bought a piece myself. The trouble is the price is higher than I'm willing to pay, but Jack needed a favor. Now Jack *could* have obtained it legitimately, but he'd have to borrow a great sum of money to do it which would put him into debt for many, many years. Which is a delightful, slow-burning revenge to extract on my enemies. But, since he's a pirate—"

"He'll do what pirates do and steal a piece, making an enemy out of the entire island of Hy-Brasil," Anise finished. "Damned if he does, damned if he doesn't."

"Precisely. I am not a subtle person, but *occasionally* I can set up a trap."

"You have a vicious streak in you, Arty. And that fight between Jack and Heliotrope?"

"Oh, *that*. I didn't even know about *that*. That's just a nice little bonus as far as I'm concerned."

"What did she *do* to you?" Anise asked. Frankly they were shocked by Arty's attitude.

Arty frowned, carefully thinking over their words before answering. "My home—my people, were at war with the fae courts long, long before I was born. We loved to say the iron is in our hands and in our souls. I was apprehensive when I first met the fae, but they seemed like *people*. Different from the people back home, but still people and they were all so much *fun*; the Autumn Court showed me a world of possibility I had never even considered. And then I fell in love."

Arty paused, their voice had started to shake and they took a moment to get a handle on their emotions before continuing. "It was a new passion and it burned as hot as a star, and I think…I think the intensity scared Heliotrope. She wanted a season's dalliance, I wanted a life together. Instead of telling me how our desires were mismatched she discarded me, spread lies about me and made it impossible for me to travel the Autumn Court safely. I lost a great many friends because of her lies. And that…that was not an appropriate response." The words were exact. Precise. Anise could tell they succinctly and accurately summarized the truth but there was a world of pain in this story which they were holding back.

"Arty, I'm so sorry. Would you like a hug?"

"…yes." Anise stepped forward, hugged Arty, and for a minute the two friends just stood there, one supporting the other.

"I'm still bitter about it."

"I know, Arty."

"Revenge is nice, though."

"I know, Arty."

"You can stop hugging me now."

Anise stepped back, keeping their hands on Arty's shoulders, and looked into their gray eyes. "Are you going to be okay?"

"Eventually. Work will help."

"You'll reach out to me or Teal if you need anything."

"By iron and stone, woman, for five centuries I have lived as the master of metalcraft! I am perfectly capable of taking care of myself!"

"I know, but you forget to eat sometimes and that makes you sad and then you hide and stare at your books all day."

"I will let you or Teal know if I need anything," Arty finally admitted, clearly wanting this conversation to be over.

"Good night, Arty." Anise smiled and unbolted the door. They were already closing when they heard Arty's response.

"Good night, *philia*."

Beloved friend. Arty didn't get much more emotional than that. Anise smiled to themselves and pulled the door shut. It was a beautiful night in Aelelea and there were so many impossible things ahead.

Super Date

Ash checked her phone for what felt like the thousandth time and saw what she'd been waiting for.

I'm here! :)

The message from Moss had arrived just a minute ago. Ash looked around the crowded restaurant for Moss's characteristic dark green hair and waved one she saw them. them. Moss smiled, waved back, and started navigating between the tables to join Ash. *Okay, just play it cool, Ash. First date with the cute enby from your chemistry class*, Ash told herself as she tore strips from her paper napkin. *Just a normal dinner and movie date. Oh God, I'm so nervous.*

"Hey you, hope I haven't kept you waiting long," Moss slid into the opposite seat of the booth and put their phone in their handbag. "The streetcar was *so* crowded, you wouldn't believe."

"Yeah, I think the football club has a game against Franklin State tonight. A lot of people in my philosophy class were talking about it. But maybe the movie theater won't be crowded?"

"I've been really looking forward to this next Benoit Blanc movie. Daniel Craig is just so much fun. Can you believe he used to be James Bond?"

"Hey there, my name's Trish I'll be taking care of you today."

A waitress walked up to their booth and placed two menus on the table. She was probably mid-thirties with purple hair and a sleeve tattoo of a team of six Pokémon. When Trish caught Moss staring she smiled and said, "I beat the Elite Four with that team back in '99. Can I get you started with some drinks or maybe appetizers?"

"Can I get a Dr. Pepper, please?" Moss asked. Ash made a mental note to herself about Moss's preference, thought that was weird, tried to erase the mental note and failed.

"How about you, hon?"

"Uh, just a coke for me, please."

"All right, I'll give you a couple minutes to look over the menu and be back with your drinks."

"I've never eaten here before," Moss said. "Do you know what's good?"

"I used to come here a lot with my mom when I was younger. Their pizzas are really good, it's a wood-fired brick oven but they only have one oven so it takes a while to make them. I usually get pasta. Or a salad."

"What on earth is an Impastabowl?"

"It's about five pounds of pasta, you get to pick the pasta and the sauce, but you have to eat the entire thing in an hour. My dad did it once on my birthday." Technically it had been a week *after* her birthday when her dad finally stopped working enough to spend time with her. "Mom and I played *Galaga* while he ate."

"Well I don't know if I'm *that* hungry. I could go for a hoagie, though."

"I've never had one of their-" Her reply was cut off by a crash of broken glass and a cacophony of screams. Ash and Moss both looked around and saw a cloud of green gas billowing from five tables away. Ash put her phone in her pocket and took Moss's hand, leading them towards the emergency exit. "We need to go. Now."

"I don't understand, what's happening?"

"It's…family history. I'll explain outside." She and Moss wove through the panicking diners and were almost to the door when a brass device sailed through the window and landed almost directly at Ash's feet. It immediately began releasing its own plume of green gas. "Goddamnit, almost made it out that time," Ash swore before she lost consciousness.

* * *

"Ash? Ash? Are you okay? Please wake up. I have no idea what's going on and I'm so scared right now."

Ash groaned and opened her eyes, blinking against the fluorescent light. "Moss? Moss, are you okay? Did they hurt you?"

"No, I'm fine. At least, I think I'm fine. You know, aside from being manacled in a secret lair."

Ash's eyes focused as she took in her surroundings. As secret lairs went it was pretty standard. Ash could tell it was an underground lair due to the stalactites and stalagmites scattered about and wondered briefly if there was somewhere you could buy them in bulk because there were no caves underneath Losantiville. Across from them was an interrogation chair that wouldn't have looked out of place in a Spanish Inquisition dungeon, and would have looked more intimidating if she hadn't recognized it from BDSM Etsy. On the far side of the lair was a computer setup that looked like something out of *Next Generation*—so what the early nineties thought the future would look like.

"Well this could be anybody's lair," Ash said. "First thing to do is get out of these manacles."

"Ash, you're taking this remarkably well," Moss said.

"I've had this happen to me before."

"Really?"

"Yeah, dozens of times."

"Ash, that's not normal."

Ash sighed internally. "Do you remember a superhero know as the Phoenix?"

"The Phoenix? I don't know anybody in Losantiville who hasn't heard of the Phoenix! I grew up with comic books about him!"

"Yeah, well. He was my dad."

There was a pause as Moss digested this fact and Ash felt her stomach sink as the familiar glow of hero worship began to shine in their eyes. "So. Your dad."

"Yeah, I don't normally bring it up on the first date because suddenly it becomes about my dad rather than me, you know? Either they're fans of the Phoenix and want to know all the nitty-gritty details or they hate my dad because he crushed their car in a fight against Professor Cephalopod and their insurance wouldn't cover a replacement."

"Has that happened?"

"Yeah. By far the most awkward date I've been on." Ash paused and thought for a second. "Well, this one is probably more awkward now."

"I don't know, I accidentally made out with my cousin."

"You did what?"

"Okay, so it turned out my great-grandfather had *two* families and we didn't know about each other. It turned out we were like half second cousins twice-removed so it wasn't a sin in the eyes of God and man but it was still kind of weird?"

"What happened after that?" Ash couldn't help help but ask. Even with her unusual childhood people making out with their cousins wasn't a normal occurrence.

"She ghosted me. Happens a lot more than I'd like."

"There shall be no escape from my clutches this time, Phoenix-spawn!" A voice that simply oozed wickedness interrupted their conversation. Ash and Moss both looked up but were unable to determine where the voice was coming from. "At long last I shall have my revenge against your sire!" This was followed by maniacal laughter.

"Oh God, it's her," Ash moaned.

"Her who?" Moss asked.

"Yes indeed, it is I!" A tall, lean woman emerged from the darkness. She was dressed in a black and gray form-fitting garment that allowed her immense freedom of movement while looking stylish and deadly. Her equally black hair was shaved on one side while the rest of it was collected in a long braid hanging over her shoulder. In both hands she carried a saber.

"Hiiiiiii, Zaj," Ash said. "How've you been?"

"You know her?" Moss asked.

"She's my dad's ex."

Zaj stopped her advance, stomping her foot in frustration. "I am no such thing! I am the Phoenix's sworn enemy!"

"Oh my Gaaaaaaaaawd. Zaj, you and my dad were 'enemies,'" and here Ash put 'enemies' in air quotes, "for five whole years. You kidnapped me every, what, four months or so? Always on a holiday weekend? Always when my dad wanted to get out of a family gathering? It was really strange how it took him the entire weekend to 'rescue' me. My mom and I figured it out pretty fast." Despite her costume makeup, which made her face look like a grinning skull, both Ash and Moss could tell she was blushing.

"Enough of this, where's the Phoenix?"

"I don't know. Probably in Miami cheating on wife number two with future wife number three right now. He retired three years ago, Zaj, you should know this." Zaj avoided eye contact with Ash and she groaned in frustration. "You *did* know this!"

"He's fishing off the coast of Key West actually, last I checked."

"Zaj. We're in the Midwest. There is no physical way my father could come here and dramatically rescue me in the hour, tops, since I've been kidnapped."

"I don't know," Moss said, "How long were we knocked out?"

"Knockout Gas Compound 37, it has a half life of fifteen minutes we weren't out for more than thirty minutes," Ash explained. "Bad Guy-Brand had to develop a fast-acting knockout gas that would work on people of different ages and weights without killing anybody. Safer and more effective than general anesthetic but the trade-off is it's only effective for a very short period of time. Zaj, what is this really about?"

"I just,—you know, now that you're of age, and the fact that your dad's retired now. I thought you might want to take up the mantle and...fight me?"

"Nope. Nope nope nope." Ash shook her defiantly. "We went over this when I was packing for college and my answer was the same as it is now. I am not doing any of this mantle-taking up thing."

"Ash, you have a gift which very few people in the world have!" Zaj's voice was pleading, all hint of wicked villainy gone. "I just want to give you an opportunity to learn how to use that gift."

"I saw what that same gift did to my dad. He started to care about the gift more than he cared about anything else. He missed every one of my birthdays and more than a few Christmases. My parents drifted so far apart that they began to resent each other, and I was trapped in the middle. I don't want any of that. I just want a *normal* life. I want to go to college. I want to see movies with cute enbies. I want to get a job where I work four or five days a week and then I'm home to spend time with my loved ones. I don't want this." Ash gestured at the secret lair as much as her manacles allowed her.

"Also, I think it was very rude to kidnap me as well," Moss said.

"Well now what am I supposed to do with you?" Zaj asked.

"You could just let us go," Moss suggested.

"No, no, that lacks panache. I'd never live it down if I just let you go. I need something suitably dramatic."

"Zaj, do you want me to call someone for you to fight?" Ash asked in exasperation. "Then we can make our escape from your clutches while you're distracted."

"You can just do that?" Moss asked, incredulous.

"Superhero kids grow up with other superhero kids, some of those superhero kids become superheroes themselves. Long story short I know the Blue Blade. What time is it?"

Zaj sheathed one of her sabers and pulled back her wrist guard to reveal a Fitbit. "Little after nine-thirty."

"Yeah, he's not doing anything right now. I can probably get him to come here. Zaj, could you give me my phone? It's in my left jacket pocket. My left, not your left." Zaj awkwardly reached into Ash's pocket and retrieved her phone before handing it to Ash, who dexterously put in her PIN one-handed and searched through her contacts. There was a short ring on the speaker phone before someone answered.

"Hey, Ash, what's happening?"

"Hey, Ben, you busy tonight?"

"Just working on a paper for school. What's up?"

"Listen, Zaj kidnapped me but her regular nemesis had to call out. She needs somebody to come in dramatically so I can make an escape in the chaos. You down?"

"Sure, beats the heck out of staring at my laptop. Where you guys at?"

"You know the rent-a-lair over on West 8th Street?" Zaj said.

"Yeah! Had a fight with a guy last week over there." There was a flurry of typing across the speakerphone. "Google says I should be able to get there in about fifteen minutes."

"Perfect, thank you Ben!" Then Ash hung up. "See, you get a dramatic fight with the Blue Blade and we get to escape. Are these standard manacles or the escape-proof kind?"

Zaj shrugged. "I don't know, they came with the place. I only rented it out for the evening."

"This isn't actually your secret lair?" Moss asked.

"In this economy? Have you seen real estate prices lately? It's absolutely ridiculous. People may call me evil but at least I'm not a landlord." Zaj sheathed her other sabre and fumbled around in one of her pockets. "I should have the key here somewhere."

"Let me give it a try first." Ash removed a bobby pin from her hair and started working on the keyhole of one of her manacles. "It's more appropriate if we manage to free ourselves first."

"So…" Moss said. "You know how to pick locks as well."

"Not really," Ash said. "The standard Bad Guy-Brand Manacles come with the shoddiest possible locking mechanism.

Basically almost any object you can put inside the keyhole is guaranteed to undo the lock. It lets even an untrained six year old with a pair of scissors unlock a pair of manacles." There was a click and the manacle Ash was working on fell open. "There we go!"

"They're popular with villains but the BDSM community *hates* Bad Guy Brand," Zaj explained as Ash worked on her other manacle. "They're not fans of people escaping when they're not supposed to." Ash managed to undo her other manacle more quickly than the first and started working on Moss's.

"I have to admit, tonight certainly has been an experience," Moss said. "And this was your life growing up?"

"Yeah," Ash said. "It's fun the first couple of times. You're happy to be included in your dad's work. But after a few years the charm starts to wear off and it starts to feel like a chore. And then you grow to resent it. At least I did, I shouldn't speak for other people."

"I'm really sorry to have ruined your evening," Zaj said and actually sounded like she meant it. "I should have taken no for an answer the first time."

"Yeah, what are you, a conservative cishet white man?" Ash joked.

"Cishet, yes. Conservative man, perish the thought." Zaj smiled. "If you don't mind though, Ash, I'd like to meet up with you from time to time. Just to see how you're doing. If that isn't weird or anything?"

"I mean, kind of? I mostly know you as my dad's ex-nemesis and ex-girlfriend."

"Ah, yeah, that makes sense..."

"But! Let me finish. But we do have shared history and it wasn't all bad." Ash finished unlocking Moss's manacles and turned to Zaj. "How about you check with my mom and we'll see about having you over for Sunday dinner sometime?"

"Would your mom be okay with that?"

"There was a point where my mom blamed you for what happened to her marriage, but she's done a lot of healing since then and accepted that dad was always the problem. I mean, I don't think she'll *like* you, but I think she'll tolerate you."

A classic red alert klaxon started. Zaj ran over to the computer terminal and pounded furiously on the keyboard. "And of course, these damn computers never come with a mouse because it ruins the 'cool factor' or some damn silly thing. Come on, show me where the alert's coming from—ah, there's the Blue Blade, knocking on the front door." Zaj typed in a command and the klaxon fell silent, allowing them to hear someone pounding on a metal door somewhere above. "Do I need to prep him first or does he need a dramatic entrance?" Zaj asked.

"Ben? Oh, he's got dramatic entrances down pat, you can let him in without a briefing."

"Perfect." Zaj input another command and a door clunked open upstairs under Ben's punches. There was the clatter of boots on metal stairs and then Ben, or rather the Blue Blade, entered the lair.

"Hello, Eclipse, up to your old tricks I see. But isn't capturing damsels a little below your level?"

"Damsel! I am no such thing!" Moss protested.

"Just roll with it, we're scenery at this point," Ash whispered back.

"Perhaps, but how else can I lure the famous Blue Blade to my lair without endangering others? Your empathy shall be your own downfall!" And Zaj dramatically drew both of her swords. In response the Blue Blade drew his own sword which really did glow with an electric blue light.

"Empathy is what makes humans great as a species! We can accomplish together more than we can alone! Your selfishness shall prove to be your own downfall in the end!"

"And yet you come alone. Are you so confident of your skill with the blade?" Zaj charged and with a flash of movement she had vanished. The Blue Blade raised his sword to the guard position, scanning the corners for any signs of movement. Like a phantom, Zaj silently emerged from the shadows, ready to strike the Blue Blade down from behind. But at the last minute, his keen sense warned him, and he turned to parry both her swords with her own.

"Your skills shall not avail you, witch!" the Blue Blade said as he pushed Zaj's swords back and went for a cut to the legs. Zaj danced out of his reach and disappeared once again.

"Should we do anything?" Moss asked.

"Honestly, we can just leave at this point," Ash said. "Unless you wanted to watch the fight."

"Nah, I'm good," Moss said. "How do we get out, anyway?"

Ash pointed towards a glowing red "EXIT" sign which had, until this point, been innocuous. "Even evil lairs have to comply with fire codes, and thank God for that." The camouflaged black-painted door opened out to a set of concrete stairs that connected directly with ground level. Ash and Moss left the sound of combat behind and exited onto the street.

"Well, that was an experience," Moss said, looking around the mostly empty street. "How do we get back to Belleview?"

Ash took out her phone and pulled up the city's transit app. "Looks like if we walk two blocks east we'll hit a bus line that can take us back."

"Sounds like a plan!" Moss said and started walking in the direction Ash had indicated. Ash followed in awkward silence. They walked for a block before Ash finally spoke.

"Moss, listen, I'm sorry that tonight kind of turned into a disaster. This is just…a side effect of my life. Sometimes supervillains burst in and my whole life goes sideways for a bit and I lose a weekend because of shenanigans. I understand if you never want me to speak with you ever again."

Moss looked at Ash and she averted her eyes, unable to take the full brunt of eye contact with them. There was another awkward silence. Ash could feel entire life forms growing, evolving, and being wiped out by asteroids in the length of that pause. And then she heard Moss laugh.

"Ash, I had a *wonderful* time," they said grinning from ear to ear. "I mean, it was pretty scary at first but the way you just sort of handled everything put me at ease. It actually got kind of fun after a while. I just wish they'd let us eat dinner before we got kidnapped."

"Well, we missed our movie but Red Rose doesn't close until midnight. We can still get you a hoagie if you'd like."

"I think I'm hungry enough to eat an entire Impastabowl at this point!" Moss laughed and then they leaned forward and kissed Ash. "How about we try to see Benoit Blanc next week?"

"Sounds good to me." Ash smiled and took Moss's hand as they started walking towards the bus stop again.

"Hey, Ash, when Zaj said you had a gift, what did she mean by that exactly."

"Uh, okay so you know how the Phoenix has superpowers?"

"Oh my gosh, do you have superpowers too? Will you show me sometime?"

Ash stopped and bit her lip, thinking for a minute. After everything that had happened tonight, Moss was asking questions about her. Not about Zaj or her deadbeat dad or if she knew the Moon Princess, but *her*. Her bastard of a high school boyfriend had only been interested in getting close to the Phoenix, and most of her other dates hadn't been much better. But Moss, adorable little Moss, didn't seem to care about any of that. Maybe, just maybe, they were worth sharing this with.

"Actually, I can show you right now," she said. "How do you feel about skipping the bus?"

"What are you going to do?"

Ash wrapped one of her arms around Moss's waist and with her other hand maneuvered both of Moss's arms to her shoulders. "Let me show you," she said, giving Moss an impish grin.

As they rose into the air and flew through the night sky, all Ash could hear was Moss's bright laughter.

About the Author

Writer, historian, ferroequinologist, numismatist, polymath. These and other fancy words can all be applied to Kalpar with varying degrees of accuracy. Kalpar is the pen-name of B.A. Klapper, a born and raise Cincinnatian who lives there to this day with their loving and supportive spouse. Kalpar is a non-binary individual who uses they/them pronouns.

You can connect with me on:

- https://www.thekalpar.com
- https://www.facebook.com/profile.php?id=61552351350395
- https://bsky.app/profile/thekalpar.bsky.social
- https://www.tumblr.com/blog/thekalpar

Subscribe to my newsletter:

- https://buttondown.com/Kalpar